A LOVE THAT GROWS

Jessica Farley had inherited Tamarisk Cottage, her grandparents' home in Cornwall. The property had been neglected and the daffodil fields alongside were a wilderness, but she was determined to re-start Gramps' daffodil business. When Andrew Rogers turned up at the cottage, Jessica was surprised that the boy she had so disliked when she was a child had turned into a handsome man. But why is Andrew so sceptical about her business venture, and who is deliberately sabotaging it?

*Books by Chrissie Loveday
in the Linford Romance Library:*

REMEMBER TO FORGET
TAKING HER CHANCES
ENCOUNTER WITH A STRANGER
FIRST LOVE, LAST LOVE
PLEASE STAY AWHILE

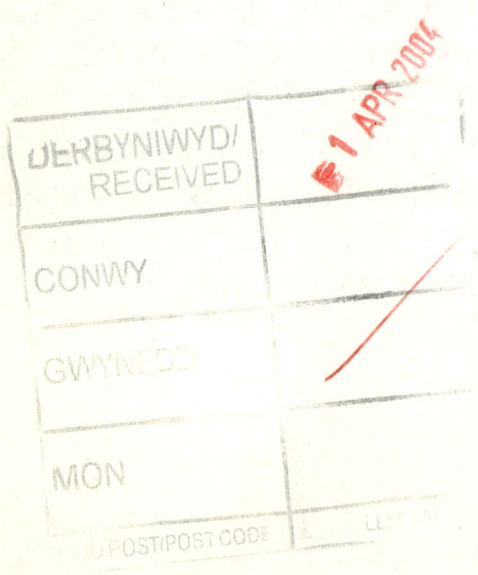

CHRISSIE LOVEDAY

A LOVE
THAT GROWS

Complete and Unabridged

LINFORD
Leicester

First published in Great Britain in 2002

First Linford Edition
published 2004

British Library CIP Data

Loveday, Chrissie
    A love that grows.—Large print ed.—
Linford romance library
    1. Floriculture—England—Cornwall—Fiction
    2. Love stories
    3. Large type books
    I. Title
    823.9'14 [F]

    ISBN 1–84395–163–0

Published by
F. A. Thorpe (Publishing)
Anstey, Leicestershire

Set by Words & Graphics Ltd.
Anstey, Leicestershire
Printed and bound in Great Britain by
T. J. International Ltd., Padstow, Cornwall

This book is printed on acid-free paper

1

The moment she had seen the envelope lying on the mat, Jessica Farley knew her life was about to change dramatically. She had stared at the envelope, intimidated by the official-looking seal on the back. This was a business letter not a personal one, with a Truro postmark. Her heart leaped. It had to be something to do with her grandparents. She hadn't been able to stop the tears falling as she carefully tore it open. She'd only been back from the funeral for a couple of days and the loss was still clawing at her senses.

Tamarisk Cottage looked just the same. In the setting sun, the honey-coloured walls took on a coppery glow. The straw thatch capped the small house with a fiery gold crown. The sea beyond it was a dark blue. At first glance, Jessica hardly noticed the dirt-streaked windows with several broken panes. The garden, once Gramps' pride and joy, was neglected and overgrown. As for the fields alongside, she could see nothing but a wilderness of dead plants all around her.

'I'm so sorry, Gramps. I'll turn it round,' she promised. 'Whatever it takes, I'll do it somehow.'

'Looks pretty desolate, doesn't it?' a voice called behind her.

She swung round. A man was leaning over the peeling gate. He had very light brown tousled hair and a tanned face.

'Do I know you?' she asked.

'You did once. Andrew Rogers.'

He held out a confident hand.

'My parents had the hotel in the village, above the port.'

'Andrew! Weren't you that pain of a child who used to torment the life out of us during the holidays?'

'Drew, everyone calls me Drew, and you are Jessica Farley, if memory serves me correctly.'

She nodded.

'Jess. Everyone calls me Jess,' she echoed his words.

He stood up straight and pushed a casual hand through his hair, brushing away a wayward strand that fell over his face. He pushed the gate open and walked over the unkempt path towards her. He was several inches taller than Jess and she found herself looking up into the clearest blue-grey eyes she had ever seen. Could that young boy whom she had disliked intensely really have turned into this handsome man?

'What's going to happen to this place?' he asked casually.

'I'm going to do it up and run it as a daffodil farm, of course, just as it always has been.'

Drew roared with laughter.

'You? You are going to farm this mess? It hasn't made a profit for years. In fact, it's made a huge loss for as long as I've . . . well, for a very long time.'

'I don't know why you should find it funny. I was brought up here. I always used to help Gramps with the picking, between school. Anyway, if you'll excuse me, I need to get myself settled before it gets dark. As you can see, I've only just arrived.'

Despite her initial attraction, she was beginning to feel irritated with this man. She had so wanted her arrival to be a special time. It would doubtless imprint on her memory for many years to come, the return to Tamarisk Cottage.

'I'll give you a hand with unloading your car,' Drew said.

He didn't ask if she would like him to help. He assumed she would accept his offer, gratefully no doubt.

'I can manage, thanks. I'm sure you have things to do. Good evening.'

Irrationally cross, she turned to the door and walked purposefully towards it. She grovelled in her bag for the keys. The solicitor had sent them to her and she knew she had put them in her bag. In desperation, she tipped the entire contents of her capacious bag on to the doormat, squatting down to rummage through her possessions. She was aware that this annoying man was standing behind her. He leaned down, lifting the edge of the mat and tipping her belongings to one side.

'There's a key here,' he said, holding it up for her to see.

'How did you know?' she gasped.

'It's always been left there. Everyone around here leaves their keys under the mat.'

'But the cottage has been empty for ages.'

'Mrs Trevaskis has been going in to clean regularly. The key was left out for her.'

'Excuse me, but how do you know so much about my affairs?' she demanded to know.

'I make it my business to know what's going on. Now, if you'd like me to help you unpack your car, I will. I suggest we get on with it. It will be getting dark in a short while.'

He turned and went out of the gate

and along the lane a short way until he reached her car. Jess watched him, nonplussed. Why on earth was he interfering with her arrangements? She'd wanted . . . needed, a few moments of quiet, a few moments to remember and grieve. Now this man had come along and spoiled it all for her. As a boy he had been a bully. He obviously hadn't changed much. She almost ran after him and childishly snatched away the various carrier bags he was carrying.

'Thanks all the same, but I can manage.'

She staggered slightly, weighed down by the bulky assortment. Halfway along the path, one bag burst, showering the path with potatoes and carrots.

'Blast!' she breathed.

'I said I'd help. Now, why don't you unlock the door and put the lights on? I'll bring the rest in and, yes, I'll even pick up the potatoes.'

Infuriating man, Jess thought. He was much too calm and controlled. He also seemed to know just a bit too much about her, for her own comfort. She wanted a quick curse and even a little scream at this particular point. Frowning, she pushed the key into the lock and turned it.

The door swung open and she stepped inside. It seemed such a long time since she'd been inside Tamarisk Cottage. She felt desperately guilty that she hadn't had more time to spend with her beloved grandparents. Gran had died almost two years ago and Gramps had stayed on, managing as best he could. He'd finally had to go into hospital before he died.

'I'm so sorry, Gramps. I should have come down during the summer. I was just so selfish,' she murmured.

He wouldn't let anyone tell her that he was in hospital. By the time she found out, it was all too late. She and her younger sister, Emily, had come down for the funeral. There had been no time to visit the cottage, so far away from the hospital. Besides, there had been some fuss over executors and estate duties to sort out and the solicitor had said it was not accessible. It now smelled cold, damp, fusty. It wasn't Gran's and Gramps' smell at all. She tried to work out what could have been missing — baking, warmth, lavender drying over the kitchen range.

'Can't you find the light switch?' Drew asked irritably. 'Just inside the door, on the left, I believe.'

'The power isn't switched on,' Jess told him, 'and I do know where the light switch is. In case you've forgotten, I lived here for most of my life.'

He dumped the bags he was carrying in a heap near the door. He went over to the fuse box, knowing exactly where to look and pushed the switch. The light came on, throwing a dim glow over the dark room.

'Bit gloomy, isn't it?' Drew suggested. 'Maybe you could find some table lamps or something. Then we shall be able to see where we are.'

'Thanks for your help, Mr Rogers,

but I can manage perfectly well now.'

He smiled and continued to unload the car and bring her things inside. She didn't know how to stop him. Truth to tell, she was rather ashamed of her erratic packing. In desperation, every plastic carrier, refuse sack, box, the lot, had been drafted into service. Somewhere at the bottom of the car were a couple of suitcases. Packed very early on, they contained her smarter clothes, a very small part of her wardrobe.

'Phew,' Drew said as he brought in the suitcases. 'I hope you have a working kettle somewhere amongst this lot. If I don't get a coffee soon, I'll probably pass out. Then I'll sue for damages.'

Despite herself, she had to acknowledge that he had saved her a great deal of time. She went into the tiny kitchen and looked around. It looked suspiciously empty. No kettle, microwave, pots or pans. In fact, the whole place looked as if it had been stripped bare. She returned to the main room. No television, ornaments or even Gran's old silver tea service, she noticed.

'Everything's gone. There must have been a break-in. Even the kettle's gone. I can't make you any tea. There's nothing to make it with.'

Foolishly, she felt very close to tears. Drew came over to her and put his arms round her, drawing her close to his chest.

'Hey, it's all right,' he whispered gently.

She stiffened, wanting to resist, but he felt so warm and comforting, so strong. She leaned into his body and allowed herself to be comforted. She could smell the scent of his soap and her cheeks brushed against the rough wool of his sweater. He lifted her face and wiped away her tears with a soft stroke of his thumb.

'Don't worry, Jess. We'll go to my place and call the police, though perhaps we should check with Mrs Trevaskis first. It could be that she put things away for safety.'

'There's nowhere to put it. I'm so sorry,' she said with a sniff. 'I never cry like this. It's just coming home here and . . .'

Her voice tailed off.

'I know exactly what it is. It's a shock. You've had a very upsetting time. Come on now. I'll take you in my car. It's parked just a little way down the lane.'

Childlike, she followed him; locking the door behind her and this time pocketing the key. His car was large and very luxurious compared to her own rather elderly heap. It smelled of expensive leather and somehow, very masculine. She glanced at him. She would never have recognised the boy she'd once known.

This man was very good looking, so different from the spotty child she remembered. He exuded confidence and purpose. Undoubtedly, any woman would be delighted to be with him. His clothes were immaculate, even allowing that he had been picking up potatoes from the garden path and hauling in endless sacks of her belongings. His designer jeans fitted extremely well, showing off his long legs. She felt ashamed, thinking of such things at this time.

'What's the matter?' he asked, noticing her expression.

'I was wondering how you managed to look so calm and neat after all your efforts,' she lied.

She caught sight of her reflection in the car window. She looked a total mess and had several dirty marks on her face. Her jeans were grubby after the long drive and the T-shirt she wore was definitely past its best.

'Do you still live at the hotel?' she asked, dreading the thought of having to walk through some reception area looking quite so dishevelled.

'Yes. My parents have retired, of course. They moved to near Falmouth. They preferred to be away from the stormy coast.'

'I'm a bit scruffy for the hotel. I'd

hate to spoil the ambience for your visitors.'

He smiled laconically.

'I don't run it as a hotel.'

'Oh? So what is it then?'

'Just my home and office. It was too good a spot to leave and I didn't fancy sharing it with hordes of tourists.'

'So, what do you do?'

He avoided her question, as they drew up in front of the huge, stone-built building. Jess looked around her. It was a long time since she had been in the village, probably a couple of miles by road from Gramps' cottage. All the signs for the hotel had been removed and the entrance was fenced off. She turned to look over the darkened sea and watched the waves crashing on to the beach. The salty tang in the air carried her right back to childhood holidays.

'Come on in. I'll get some hot tea organised and then we'll make some phone calls.'

'I'm very grateful,' Jess began.

She stopped. Why on earth had she allowed herself to be dominated like this? He had virtually taken over and ordered her around. She had a perfectly good phone at the cottage, and even if that didn't work, she had her mobile phone. Drew left the room and she heard him opening doors somewhere. She looked around. The large lounge had once been for guests but now, it was an elegant room in a large house. Obviously, Drew Rogers was very successful, whatever he did.

'Tea's on its way,' Drew announced as he came back into the room. 'Now, I'll find Mrs Trevaskis' number and we'll see what's been going on. You can always stay here if there's a problem. Something I have in plenty, spare rooms.'

'Look, it's very kind of you but I can manage, really. I'll have some tea and then I must get back to my cottage. It's getting late and I've had a long drive.'

She hesitated, realising that she had called it her cottage for the very first time. The words felt alien to her.

'It's cold, damp and hasn't been lived in for ages. Besides, everything that makes life comfortable has been removed. Now, here's the number.'

He picked up the phone and dialled. Jess perched on a chair, staring out of the window. The light was fading fast.

'Hello? Mrs Trevaskis? It's Drew Rogers. I'm calling on behalf of Jess Farley. Yes, that's right.'

Jess came back from her daydream, realising she was once more letting him take over. She rose from her seat and crossed the room. Drew was deep in conversation and she waited beside him.

'I see. OK. I'd better call the police then. Thank you. 'Bye.'

He put the phone down.

'It seems that you probably have been burgled. Everything was there last time she went in.'

'I can't believe it. How could anyone be so ruthless? It's horrible.'

'You couldn't have had a worse

homecoming if you'd tried. I'm so sorry.'

'If the key was always left out, it was easy for anyone to get in. I suppose everyone knew it was there. When did Mrs Trevaskis last visit?'

'She hasn't been in this week. She didn't realise you were coming so soon.'

'I didn't know myself,' Jess grumbled. 'I had intended to work a month's notice but once my boss knew I was leaving, he decided I should leave immediately.'

'Nice boss,' Drew put in.

'Oh, he's all right. I got a month's pay anyway. I gave notice at my flat and there seemed to be nothing to keep me. With winter coming on, I knew I needed to get down here and begin some planting, if there's to be a crop next spring.'

'You're serious, aren't you?'

'Of course. I owe it to them to try to work the farm.'

'But your grandfather hadn't grown a successful crop of daffs since your gran died. He just couldn't seem to get his act together.'

Jess felt tears pricking at the back of her eyes again. She hadn't realised how bad things were. He'd always sounded so cheerful when she phoned. The final weeks in the nursing home had worried her but there was nothing she could do. She'd been working abroad, on and off, for several months. It was all she could do to cram in the odd visit. She should have realised things were bad.

'In fact,' Drew continued, 'I know he was thinking of selling up. His health had been letting him down. He knew it was a lost cause, if the truth be told.'

'I'm still curious as to your involvement. How do you know so much, things I, his grand-daughter and heir, didn't know?'

He avoided answering as a woman knocked at the door and brought in an elegantly laid tray of tea.

'Mrs Jamieson, my housekeeper,' he introduced.

The two women nodded at each

other. The tray was put on a table near to Drew and Mrs Jamieson left the room.

'You didn't answer my question, Drew,' Jess continued. 'How do you know so much about Gramps and his intentions?'

'This is a small place. Any business-man will be aware of what goes on. Milk and sugar?'

'Just milk, thanks. And that's what you are? A businessman?'

'Scone? I can recommend them. Mrs J. makes the best scones I've ever tasted.'

Jess glared at him. What was he trying to hide? There was something very odd about the way he kept changing the subject and avoiding giving any answers.

'I think we'd better phone the police,' he announced, once her mouth was full of scone. 'Then I'll take you to meet them back at the cottage. I mentioned to Mrs J. that you may be staying the night here, and she's preparing a room for you. I can't let you stay in that cold, dreary cottage in the circumstances.'

'Look, you've been very kind but I'd like to get back now. I do have my mobile phone, so I'm not cut off. Once the range is lit, the place will soon warm up. I'd be grateful for a lift back. Thanks for your help and the tea.'

Jess replaced her empty cup on the tray.

'If you don't mind?'

She went to the phone and dialled triple nine.

'Police, please. Oh, sorry, I didn't know. Thanks.'

She put her hand over the mouth-piece.

'Apparently I should have dialled another number to report a burglary.'

'I would have told you,' Drew said annoyingly.

'Hello? Yes.'

She reported the details and agreed to wait at the cottage until they arrived.

'So, if you don't mind taking me

home? I don't fancy the cliff walk in the dark.'

He shrugged and put down his cup. Without a word he followed her outside and drove her back. The short journey was made in virtual silence.

'Would you object to me waiting with you?' he asked, as they pulled up outside the dark, isolated cottage.

'It's all right, I can manage. You've been very kind but I mustn't keep you any longer. I'm sure you must have things to do.'

'Nothing,' he said cheerfully. 'Besides, I haven't given up on persuading you to come back to my place for the night. Mrs J. will cook us dinner and then you could relax, have a hot bath, listen to music or watch TV. Whatever you fancy.'

Jess considered his words. He made it sound very tempting, but she felt a sense of disloyalty to her grandfather. He had left his whole property to her, lock stock and barrel. If she abandoned it at the first problem, what chance did she stand of making a success of the business?

'Thanks all the same, but I'd prefer to stay here. Start as I mean to go on. You've been very kind.'

She leaned over to open the car door, but he leaned across her, determined to do even this small task for her. She smelled again his clean, male scent and her heart jumped unexpectedly. He half turned, so that his mouth was fractions of an inch away. He hesitated for a moment and then placed a gentle kiss on her cheek.

'For old times' sake,' he whispered.

She was so surprised she almost froze. Then she relaxed, realising that it was very pleasant. In fact, she'd rather enjoyed being kissed by this man. Her heart began to pound and a strange surge of longing took over her. It was such a long time since anyone had kissed her like that, since anyone had kissed her at all. She had plenty of male friends from work, but none of them was at all special, romantically.

'I'm sorry,' Drew said as he pulled away from her. 'I don't know what made me do that.'

Jess was temporarily breathless. She felt very peculiar inside and could not quite explain why. She tried to pull herself together and make light of the incident.

'I have to say, I'm not used to kissing total strangers.'

'But we're not strangers. I think we even went to the same school for a time, before I got packed off to boarding school.'

'All the same,' Jess protested, 'we haven't met since we grew up. I would never have known you.'

The exchange was broken off as she saw the flash of a blue light coming along the lane.

'The police are coming,' she said in a voice that was curiously husky.

'I'll leave you to it then, if you're sure,' Drew said, re-starting his engine. 'I'll maybe see you tomorrow. I'll be up around nine thirty. I'll bring breakfast, if you can wait that long.'

'There's no need,' Jess began to protest, but he had pulled the door to and was reversing along the lane. She took a deep breath and waited for the policeman to follow her up the path.

For the next hour, she gave as many details as she could to the officer. Her list of missing items was somewhat sketchy as she was unaware of exactly what had been left in the cottage. Obviously, he would want to question Mrs Trevaskis to establish her movements and hopefully, list the missing items more accurately.

'Now, miss, is there someone you'd like us to contact to stay with you? It's a lonely spot this. You haven't got much in the way of home comforts, have you?'

'I'll be fine, officer, thanks. Once I get the range going, the place will soon warm up.'

'If you're sure. I'll get the patrol car to look in on you, when he passes during the night. There's not a lot more

I can do now. We'll call on Mrs Trevaskis in the morning. If you're certain you're OK, I'll be on my way.'

'I am, thanks. You've been very kind.'

'Just one thing, miss. Make sure you don't leave keys under the mat in future, and make sure you lock up when I've left. OK?'

Jess nodded and watched as the comfortingly large man drove off, leaving her feeling very much alone. She locked the door and set about trying to work the old-fashioned range. She had been right about the sudden changes in her life. She bit her lip, wondering if she really had bitten off more than she could chew.

'I'm going to do it, Gramps,' she whispered determinedly. 'I promise.'

2

For over an hour, Jess struggled with the unwilling fire. She put in wood, firelighters, papers, everything she could think of, but nothing was going to make it light.

'Must be damp in the chimney,' she told herself.

No heat from the range meant there was no hot water and no heat in the bedrooms. It also meant there was no means of cooking anything, especially as the microwave was also missing. As she explored the cottage, she discovered that even more was missing than she had realised. Everything remotely portable had gone. Only the large, old-fashioned furniture was left. Someone with a large van must have cleared the place. The cottage was so tucked away, that anyone could have taken their time to remove whatever they wanted.

She slumped down in a chair, pulling her coat down over her knees. It was freezing. Why had she been so stubborn? If she phoned Drew, she was certain his offer would still be open. She smiled as she remembered his kiss. It had been unexpected, warm and undoubtedly exciting. She shivered again. It would be foolish to stay here, in this freezing cold, uninhabitable cottage.

She picked up her bag to find her mobile phone. Even that seemed to have gone missing. She must have dropped it on the mat when she had been hunting for the keys. She pulled the door open and searched around the doormat. There was no sign of it. Where on earth could it be? She tried to think of the last time she'd used it. It certainly hadn't been today.

'Ah, well,' she called to the night sky, 'just another little set-back. So what? I'm good at coping. Everyone says so.'

The first drops of rain fell from the

sky and she groaned. She shut the door firmly and went into the sitting-room. The electric fire had gone but the fireplace was still useable. She took some sticks and paper and tried to lay a fire. They soon caught and she added some logs she'd brought in from the store. It looked much more cheerful with a blaze going, even if it didn't give out a lot of heat. She would manage, she told herself. She could bring some blankets in here and sleep on the sofa for the night.

Tomorrow things would soon be looking better. She would phone the insurance company and easily replace the essentials. If she ignored her rumbling stomach and made do with the remains of her picnic lunch, she could last till the morning. Anyhow, Drew had promised to call, complete with breakfast. She munched on a couple of biscuits and settled down for the night. Hardly the way she had planned to spend the first night back here!

Exhausted by the journey, she fell into a deep sleep. She awoke with a start, some hours later. She felt disorientated and confused. Something must have woken her but everything was silent now. The logs had burned away and she shivered. She was snuggled down among several blankets, unwilling to lose the little warmth she had. She glanced at the luminous dial of her watch. It was three o'clock — several hours till dawn. She tried to sleep again but it would not come. There was a sudden crash, from somewhere upstairs. She stiffened and hardly dared breathe. There was definitely something or someone up there. Perhaps the burglars had returned.

Carefully, she climbed out of her cocoon of blankets and felt her way across the room. She pulled the door open, wincing at every creak of the old frame. Stealthily, she crept up the old staircase, the smooth banister familiar beneath her fingers. The noises were coming from her grandparents' old room. She flung the door open, reaching for the light switch as she did so. To her horror, several rats scurried for hiding places.

She shuddered as she watched them, disturbed from their evening's entertainment. They had obviously been nesting somewhere in the room and she looked around, dreading to see where they'd been. There was nothing obvious, so she returned to the sitting-room where the temperature was marginally less Arctic. Now there's something else to be added to her list of jobs for the next day — rat extermination.

Weary though she felt, sleep was over for the night. She should try to light the fire again. She longed for a cup of hot coffee, wondering how long it would be before Drew returned. She hoped he'd bring at least a Thermos with him. She cursed herself for not bringing her own kettle with her. She had left it, along with other necessities, for the next tenant, certain that everything she might need would be in place at the cottage.

The wretched fire would not light again. Whatever she used as kindling, burned away in a few seconds, but not before it had sent a cloud of black smoke into the room. She went into the kitchen again and made another attempt to get the range to start. Useless. How had Gran managed it all those years? Surely it couldn't be beyond her abilities. Suppressing a shiver, she found a piece of paper in her bag and began to make a list.

'Nothing like a list to make you feel positive,' she told herself, and began to write.

1. **Contact chimney sweep.**
2. **Phone insurance about replacements for stolen goods.**
3. **Shopping.**
4. **Rat catcher.**
5. **Find mobile phone.**

She looked at the list. Number Five had better become Number One, she thought. She felt more miserable than she could ever remember. She had been utterly mad to drive down here without even telling anyone. Nor had she thought to check that everything was in order. She had convinced herself that she was coming home. It would be almost the same as it always had been. This cottage had been home. This was where she and Emily had been brought up by their grandparents, following the deaths of their parents.

Emily had moved away at the first chance and had rarely returned. She thought of her sister, so pretty, self-assured and competent. Jess had been troubled for many days when she had learned that she was the sole heir to their grandparents' daffodil farm. She felt badly that Emily hadn't been left anything more than a few trinkets. There was no money involved, just a rundown, failing wreck of a business. Emily had horrified Jess when she suggested selling immediately, to the highest bidder, adding something about them both going on a cruise. But she had only been joking, Jess thought and hoped.

It began to get light around seven-thirty. Jess went outside to look again for her mobile phone. She went out to the car, hoping it may have been dropped there, but found nothing. It was completely, mysteriously, lost.

'Drat!' she muttered. 'Another chore to do.'

With no other means of contacting anyone, she'd have to go down to the village and use the phone box. With her current run of luck, it would probably be out of order. It would probably be a couple of hours before Drew arrived. She should make a start on some unpacking. She glanced in the mirror.

Good grief, she thought, I should do something about the way I look.

If Drew saw her like this, he'd no more want to kiss her than fly to the moon. Not that she really cared, of course. He was just an old acquaintance who had been kind. The kiss had meant nothing more than his attempt to cheer her up. She closed her eyes, remembering, trying to convince herself.

He was a powerful, confident man who seemed to have been successful at whatever it was he did. She mustn't let him think she was going to rely on him for anything. She would accept his offer of breakfast gratefully, only because things were so bad here. That would be it then. Once she was getting things moving again, she would never need to bother him again.

After a wash at the kitchen sink, where the water seemed marginally colder than ice, she felt wide awake. She began to make a list of things she needed to buy urgently. It was like starting everything from scratch. She was constantly pushing away tears, as she looked for remembered treasures which were now missing. There had been nothing of any great value, but how did one replace a lifetime of memories?

Drew arrived soon after nine. He carried a large box and looked neat and well-groomed.

' 'Morning,' he called cheerily. 'Sleep well?'

'Not bad, considering,' she managed to mumble, hoping he didn't notice just how scruffy she was looking.

'It isn't very warm in here. I'd have thought you'd have the range going by now.'

'I think the chimney must be blocked,' she said half-heartedly.

'Good job I brought a Thermos then, isn't it? Mrs J. has packed us a good breakfast. Bacon roll to start, or would you like some fruit?'

'I'd kill for some coffee,' Jess told him. 'Then bacon rolls sound like heaven.'

'Did you manage to cook something for supper?' he asked.

Jess shook her head.

'My, my, you really do need someone to look after you, don't you?'

'I'll be fine,' she said, suppressing another shiver. 'It's all gone a bit pear-shaped.'

He glanced into the next room as he munched his roll.

'Did you sleep down here?' he demanded. 'Why on earth did you do that?'

'I managed to light that fire. But it's gone out now and wouldn't go again, and there are rats upstairs, and I've lost my mobile.'

'You silly girl,' he said gently. 'Why on earth didn't you come back with me? Stupid pride, I suppose.'

The soft way he spoke was almost too much for her. She felt a lump growing in her throat.

'I don't bite you know, and I'm only too pleased to help. It can be very lonely around here,' he said.

'I would have come, but I felt I owed it to Gramps. If I failed right at the beginning, I should never forgive myself. These rolls are wonderful, by the way.'

'There's some fruit and bread to toast, if we had a toaster, and there's local honey. We could always have bread and honey.'

He smiled.

'Sounds great.'

She ate greedily and drank the hot coffee gratefully. Things never looked quite so bleak in the morning light. When they had finished, Drew packed everything back in the box.

'I have several suggestions to make,' he said authoritatively. 'You can come down to my place and have a bath or shower, whatever you like. Then you can use the phone to get things moving. Presumably, you have an insurance policy? You should be able to get some new stuff immediately, or, I can probably lend you whatever you need. We kept a lot of the hotel stuff when we stopped trading. I think there are about forty kettles for a start. They weren't worth selling for the little you get. How does that sound?'

'Brilliant. It's very generous of you. I can't think why you are being so kind to me.'

'My pleasure. I just happened to be in the right place at the right time.'

She thought about his words. Had he known when she was arriving? It was extremely opportune that he was up on this lonely stretch of cliff top just at the right moment, almost as if he'd been waiting for her. She pushed the unwelcome thought away.

'I suppose you haven't got the odd, spare mobile lying around? Gramps had a fax and phone combined, obviously useful to our thieves. I can't think what I could have done with my own phone.'

He reached into his jacket pocket and handed her a mobile.

'Use this for now. I'm sure I have another somewhere.'

'Oh, but I couldn't. I was only joking.'

'No, I insist. You can't be without the means of contacting the outside world, unless, of course, you take up my offer to come and stay at my place. Think about it, Jess.'

He put his hand on her arm as he was speaking. It was a careless gesture, but it felt as if a jolt of electricity shot through her. She stared at him. It didn't seem to have affected him and she tried to turn away as if nothing had happened. She felt aware of his eyes burning into her back. She felt unsettled. She wanted to feel his comforting arms around her again, just as he had done last night. She brushed away the thoughts. It had only been a friendly, human gesture. She was obviously so tense inside that she was letting her imagination run away with her.

'I must pay for the calls at least.'

'Forget it. You're not going to spend hours talking to Australia or anything. We're talking pence here. Forget it, I say.'

His hand was still holding her arm. She imagined herself held firmly against his powerful body, feeling his breath against her cheek. It felt good, in her imagination. She looked into his clear grey eyes, unusual eyes, almost silver-looking this morning.

'Thanks very much then. I accept.'

Her words sounded squeaky and her breath felt ragged.

'You know, I . . . that kiss last night,' he said suddenly.

Jess's heart stopped beating for a second and her knees felt so weak, she needed to sit down.

'I'm sorry?' she mumbled.

'Don't take away all my pride. You can't have forgotten.'

'No, of course not,' she stammered.

'I'd like to try again, in less difficult circumstances.'

He reached over to her and pulled her closer. Her eyes closed as she waited for his warm lips to touch her own. She nestled against his body, feeling warm and safe. His arms held her tightly, as if he was unwilling to let go in case she left him again. His kiss was sweet and gentle. The warmth from his body felt very good.

'Oh, Jess,' he murmured. 'I'm so glad you came back.'

He kissed her again, until she began to feel quite dizzy. His hand moved to pull her even closer to him.

'Please give up this nonsense about living here. There's plenty of room at my place. Your grandfather wouldn't want you to be under any obligation. You can even have your own apartment, if you really want it.'

'Drew, please, hold on. We've only just met. You can't make these sort of suggestions. Besides, I want to live here. I owe it to my grandparents.'

His eyes hardened, like slate, Jessica thought. He let her go, and she almost staggered back at the swiftness of his movement.

'Drew, I'm sorry, I wasn't rejecting you. I just don't want to be pressured. I have a lot to sort out here. I'd like us to be friends.'

He stared at her for several moments.

Then he gave a shrung.

'Sorry. Maybe I was rushing things. I was foolish. I always make up my mind very quickly. When I want something, I go after it immediately. I got it wrong. I suppose I misread your signals.'

'I wasn't aware that I was giving any signals,' Jess protested.

Her heart was pounding, belying her words. This man was exactly her sort of man, tall, handsome, bright and evidently highly successful. All the same, if she rushed into things, how could she make the right choices? Instinct and attraction were in conflict. However tempting his offer, she knew that she had something to prove. If nothing else, she needed to prove to herself that she could make a success of her grandparent's business.

'Drew,' she said softly, 'I really would like us to be friends, very much.'

He moved towards her again and held her arms.

'I want it, too. I suppose I wanted more.'

He kissed her cheek, without any of the warmth and passion he had shown earlier.

'I'd better leave you to your problems. You can use the phone as much as you need. You can return it later, when you've got the land line fixed.'

'Thanks very much, and thank you again for breakfast. It was most welcome.'

She spoke to his retreating form. He was already halfway up the path. Somehow, she felt that Mr Drew Rogers was not willing to wait for anything. Maybe she had messed things up with him, but she knew it was the right thing to do. She watched him drive away and went back into her cottage. It was still cold and unwelcoming. The luxury that Drew offered seemed a million miles away. With a sigh, Jess collected the phone book and began to search for the help she needed so desperately.

For the next two days, the little cottage was a hive of activity. The sweep came and dislodged several birds' nests from the chimneys and several bags of soot. The pest control officer laid bait to remove the rats. Finally, once the phone was re-connected, she felt better. With a warm, functioning home again, life was less bleak. When Mrs Trevaskis came to help clean up the mess, Jess realised that the old family helper was a similar age to her grandparents. She sensed that the old lady wouldn't be able to work for much longer, even if Jess had been able to afford to employ her.

The police could find no trace of any of the stolen goods and the insurance company finally agreed to send a cheque. She was sad at the loss of so many old family treasures. At least now, she could purchase a few of the essentials. She had heard nothing more from Drew and knew that she had to pluck up courage to make contact herself. She still hoped they could be friends, but she also knew that any sort of relationship based on haste was destined to failure.

All the same, he had occupied quite a lot of her thoughts in the last few days. There was a powerful force between them. She had felt charged with a sort of energy for the brief time they were together. She picked up his mobile phone, knowing she had the perfect excuse to visit him. Besides, the battery was completely flat and she had no means of charging it. Though she had her own charger, it wasn't the same model.

She decided to walk down the steep cliff path to Drew's house. It was a beautiful, autumn day, with clear blue skies. The sea was a deep azure, with darker blue patches where the clouds left their shadows. Her heart sang with pleasure. This was the most beautiful place on earth, she thought. No wonder her grandparents had always lived here, happy with their attempts to make a simple living.

Though she still felt slightly guilty that the property was left entirely to her and not shared with her sister, Emily, it was the right thing. Emily would hate living here, so far from London and the life she wanted to lead. Jess smiled. She loved her younger sister dearly but was always totally exasperated by her attitude to life. Nothing was ever planned, nothing lasted for long. Emily had found and lost more jobs in the last five years than most people had in a lifetime.

As she rounded the corner, Jess grinned with pleasure. The little port looked at its best with the high tide. The little boats bobbed on the sea instead of lying keeled over as they did at low tide, and beaches always looked so much neater at high tide, she thought. Drew's house was the largest building in the village. The trade brought by the one-time hotel must be very much missed. A large fence blocked the old route she used to take through the hotel grounds. She clambered down the steep path and walked round to the end of the drive. Drew's car was parked outside the door. Whatever he did for a living, he was obviously able to do it from home.

Her heart was beating rather too fast as she rang the doorbell. Mrs Jamieson opened it.

'Oh, it's you,' she said with surprise. 'Can I help you?'

'I wanted to see Drew, if possible.'

'I'm not sure if he's available. I'll go and check. I suppose you'd better come in.'

Jess felt far from welcome and wondered if she had somehow offended the woman. She stood uncomfortably in the huge hall. Marble statues stood in alcoves along the sides, giving the place the air of a museum rather than a home. She wandered over to a large oil painting of some Victorian gentleman. Not at all a friendly sort of person, she thought.

'Forbidding, isn't he?' Drew's voice said behind her.

Her heart gave an unexpected jolt as she turned and saw him. He was wearing a formal suit with collar and tie.

'I am expecting a client any moment, so I can only spare a few minutes.'

'I'm sorry to disturb you. I only wanted to thank you and return your phone. Thanks very much for it. Saved my life. It needs charging, I'm afraid.'

She held it out to him.

'Oh, I found yours in my car. I meant to drop it off to you but I've been rather tied up all week. But I knew you had mine, anyhow. How are things going?'

His voice sounded formal and distant. Perhaps it was because she had caught him unexpectedly during his working day.

'You found my phone in your car? I wonder how we didn't see it earlier. I don't even remember taking my bag with me in your car.'

She frowned, trying to recall the events before she realised it was missing.

'Doesn't matter, does it? It's found

now and that's what matters. So, have you settled in now?'

'I'm getting there. At least I have the heating working and I've restored a few home comforts. Look, I'd better not keep you any longer. You're obviously trying to work. Must be difficult working at home.'

He crossed to a table and picked up her own phone, handing it to her.

'Maybe I could cook dinner for you sometime,' she suggested, 'as a thank you for your help.'

'Not necessary,' he said coolly.

Jess blushed in embarrassment. He was so completely different from the way he'd been at their last meeting. She felt hurt and snubbed. She gave a shrug and turned to leave.

'Sorry, I didn't mean to sound rude. I'll give you a call and we can maybe go out somewhere.'

He looked distracted and Jess realised that he was trying to get rid of her. Perhaps he didn't want her in the way of his meeting. If that was the way he wanted it, she'd remove herself immediately.

'OK. Thanks again. I'll get back home. 'Bye.'

She went to the door and pulled it open. It was so heavy, she needed both hands. He came closer and helped her, his arm brushing against hers and just as before, the contact seemed to give her a jolt. Drew didn't seem to have noticed anything and she hurriedly blustered her way out of his house.

'Didn't you bring your car?' he asked in surprise.

'I walked. It's such a lovely day. I wanted to get some fresh air and the exercise does me good.'

'I'd offer to drive you back but as I say, I'm waiting for a client.'

'No worries,' she called as she walked away swiftly.

She knew he was staring after her but she felt embarrassed and angry at his attitude. She stood aside as a large green saloon car swept through the wrought iron gates. It pulled up outside the house and Drew shook hands with the man who got out. Jess wondered where she'd seen the man before. He was definitely familiar. She racked her brains but she could not place him. Must have been someone from her past, she assumed.

She wandered down to the sea and stood watching the timeless waves as they rolled on to the shore. The safe shelter of the little harbour kept the heavy seas beyond the breakwater. The smell of seaweed filled her nostrils. She was truly home, in the Cornwall she loved so much.

3

Jess walked over the land that lay alongside the cottage. The field was just over ten acres and was usually filled with daffodil bulbs. She remembered the neat rows of flowers, of drying bulbs at the end of the season and finally, the ploughing and re-planting for the next year's crop. The cycle had gone on for as long as she could remember.

It was hard work but rewarding and just about profitable enough for a reasonable living. She knew there were other ways to supplement her income and she had many plans for new ventures. It was all a very long way from her work in an office. She stood in the middle of her field and stared round at the devastation. Many bulbs were still lying on the damp ground. Some were mouldy and weeds had grown unchecked over the entire plot. It was going to take a great deal of work, sooner rather than later, if she was to get anything planted before the winter. The whole field needed ploughing and whatever was left lying would have to be buried. She crossed to the shed and began to pull the covers off the old tractor.

An hour later, she rubbed filthy hands over her jeans and clambered up to the high seat of the ancient machine. She turned the key and the engine burst into life. She pounded the steering-wheel with a triumphant cry, then she put it into gear and moved forward slowly. Triumphantly, she set off across the field. At last something was going well. Though she had driven the tractor ever since she was old enough to reach the controls, she was not exactly an expert. The wheels bounced over the deep ruts and she felt shaken to bits by the time she drove it back to the shed.

She glanced at her watch. It was 'way past lunchtime and she was finished.

Tempting though it was to attach the plough and begin working on the field, she knew she must eat something. She glanced over towards the sea. There weren't many places where working commanded such a wonderful view. She saw movement in the lane alongside the field and caught a glimpse of a light green car passing. It was the same one she'd seen at Drew's place this morning.

The driver had slowed right down and was definitely looking over her hedge. He hadn't looked the type to be interested in country matters of any sort, let alone a semi-derelict daffodil farm, Jess thought. The car stopped and the driver got out. He obviously couldn't see Jess, as she stood in the shadows of the tractor shed. He came and peered over the field gate, something in his hand. It looked like a tape recorder.

As she watched, he spoke into it, looking in different directions as he spoke. She could contain herself no longer and walked briskly out of the shed, towards the intruder. He glanced at her, turned and got quickly back into his car, then drove off at speed. She was left staring after him, wondering what on earth was going on.

The clouds piled in from the west and before she had finished her snack, the first drops of rain were falling. She cursed. There was little point in trying to use the ancient plough that afternoon. She might as well go and do some more shopping. She drove to Penzance and wandered round the narrow streets. It had such character. She loved the uneven surfaces, the twisting back lanes and even the new shopping precinct.

On her way back to the carpark, she wandered down a street where there were a number of antique shops. She glanced in at the windows as she passed. Suddenly she froze. Surely that was her grandparents' silver tea service! Trembling, she went into the shop and asked to look at the item. She would know if it really was, once she looked inside. The teapot had an orange stain in it, from the day when she and her sister had used it for a dolls' tea party. The orange paint was supposed to have been juice. It was the only time she could remember Gran being really angry. Sadly, the stain had never come out. The shopkeeper gladly took the set from the window. Jess opened the lid. The orange stain was unmistakable.

'Can you tell me where you got this?' she asked in a shaky voice.

'A gentleman brought it in, some weeks ago. It's a lovely piece, isn't it?'

Jess nodded. She didn't trust herself to speak. She took a deep breath and spoke again.

'What did he look like?' she asked.

'I can't really say.'

The dealer looked distinctly defensive, Jess thought.

'Now, are you interested, or shall I put it back in the window?'

'It's too expensive for me,' Jess mumbled as she fled from the shop.

She felt at a loss. What was she to do? It most certainly was the silver that was missing. If she went to the police, she had no way to prove it. If only she had remembered the orange stain earlier. She looked in the other windows and saw a vase that she also recognised. Obviously, the thief or thieves had distributed their booty along this street.

'Well, well, we meet again,' a voice behind her said and she jumped.

'Drew! What are you doing here?'

'I often come down here to see what's around. I buy and sell the odd few pieces.'

He looked casually neat in a leather jacket, worn over immaculate jeans.

'Can I ask your advice about something?' she said.

'Sure, but don't expect me to know anything much. I only dabble.'

'My grandparents' silver tea set is in the shop down there. I know it is. But the woman wouldn't tell me where it came from.'

'I bet she wouldn't. You didn't ask her, did you?'

' 'Course I did. At first she said a man had brought it in a few weeks ago. Then she clammed up. If she was telling the truth, that must have been before Gramps died. Yet I'd have sworn it was on the inventory of the cottage, produced by the executors. I don't understand.'

'Look, I know most of the people round here. Leave it with me. I'll see what I can find out.'

'That's very kind of you, but shouldn't I tell the police? There's a vase in another shop, too. Not worth much but I definitely recognised it. It was still a part of my childhood.'

'Leave the police out of it. I would. Let me see what I can find out and I'll let you know. If I don't succeed, then we can call the police.'

He spoke with authority and she had no alternative but to do what he suggested.

'Well, if you're sure. Thanks.'

'Do you fancy some tea?' he asked.

'I ought to be getting back, really,' she replied, glancing at her watch.

'There's a shop back here that does great cream teas. Treat yourself.'

Jess laughed then replied, 'OK. Just this once.'

She reflected on his different moods. Last time they had met, he seemed distant and stand-offish. Now he was charm itself and he seemed more than willing to be friends again. She ran her fingers through her long blonde hair, purely out of habit.

'I don't think you're going to make any difference to that,' Drew remarked as he saw her gesture.

'What? Oh, my hair. I usually keep it tied back. Good for my image of the tough, outdoor girl.'

'But you're not, are you?'

'I am,' she protested, 'very tough. You don't have to be Amazon-sized to be tough.'

'If you say so, but you look rather too

feminine to be able to cope with much. In fact, you have the sort of figure most women would envy. Good for most things, except farming.'

'Are you always this personal?'

'I'm sorry. I've always had the habit of saying what I think. I'm being very rude. I really do like you, Jess. I'm afraid we got off on the wrong foot. I'd like to make it up to you, if I can. Will you have dinner with me?'

'I did offer to cook for you but you turned me down.'

'I'm sorry about that. My mind was on a particular bit of business. I wasn't thinking properly.'

'Who was the guy who visited you this morning? I'm sure I've seen him somewhere before, and then later, this afternoon, he was looking at my field with such curiosity that it made me anxious.'

'Oh, he's just an acquaintance, a business acquaintance. Now, shall I order?'

'You've never told me exactly what it

is that you do,' she said again querying him.

'All sorts. This and that.'

'You don't make serious money that way. Obviously you do have serious money.'

'I do a lot of investment work. It's all rather complicated.'

'And is the man I saw today something to do with your investments?' she persisted.

'I suppose you could say that. Look, I'd really rather not talk about it any more. I'm much more interested in your plans. After all, we're practically neighbours. How are you going to manage to make a living with daffodils, for heaven's sake? They're such a dodgy business. Working in all weathers and so much hard work. Why bother?'

'Gramps built up his business over the years. The flowers have a wholesale market. He also had a large client base for bulbs and there's even a mail-order service to private buyers.'

'Still sounds somewhat labour intensive to me, and, as I said, not very reliable with the weather and all.'

Jess knew he was talking a lot of sense. In fact, it was pretty much the line of thought she'd had herself. It was all too small to be really productive. She had a few plans to improve and expand the lines instead of relying on one crop but it was too early in the planning stages to discuss.

She was on her second scone when he leaned over. He took his napkin and removed a blob of cream that had found its way to her nose. He smiled again at her, melting every scrap of resistance she had been building up. He put a finger under her chin and drew her closer to him. He placed the lightest feather of a kiss on her lips and let her go again. She blushed and looked to see if anyone else had noticed. The afternoon tea brigade was too involved in scones and cream!

'Sorry. I've embarrassed you again,' Drew said. 'I just couldn't resist, especially not with cream on your nose.'

She cast her eyes down, not knowing what to say. Besides, her heart had taken leave of its senses again and was pounding away so hard that she was certain he must be able to hear it.

'I'm sorry. I must be out of practice, I suppose.'

She felt herself blushing even more. She was behaving like some teenager on a first date, ridiculous. Drew was almost an old school friend, even if he did keep kissing her at unlikely moments. Why did he have this effect on her?

'Is it too late to accept your invitation to dinner?' he asked.

'No, of course it isn't.'

'What time will suit you?'

'What do you mean? Tonight?'

'Why wait? If it isn't convenient, we can always go out somewhere, I'd like to take you out. There are lots of places I want to show you.'

'I'd have to do some shopping. I haven't sorted out my food stocks yet.'

'Then swallow your stubborn pride and accept my invitation. I'll pick you up at seven, and no arguments.'

'OK. Thanks,' she breathed, once more feeling light-headed.

'See you later. I'll see if I can find out anything about that silver. I suggest you keep your eyes open for any other items you've lost. You never know. I've heard car boot sales are the best places to look for stolen property. I must get on, now.'

As she drove home, Jess was deep in thought. Drew was everything she could have hoped for in a man, but there was something not quite right. He was just too perfect, too handsome, too ready to help her. She was quite potty, she told herself. If he wanted her company, he could have it. He was nice to be with and she enjoyed his company. It wasn't as if she really was a gauche teenager.

She'd lived in a city for years and knew what was what. She was not without experience with men, either. She'd had loads of casual boyfriends.

Granted, not as many as Emily. She was the pretty one, whom everyone loved. A petite blonde with big eyes that made people try to take care of her. Dear Em. She must give her a call soon and find out what she was doing.

The rain had stopped and it was almost dark when she stopped outside her cottage. There was a light on. Strange. She hadn't left a light on, she was certain. Quietly, she walked up the path and peered in at the window. The kitchen was empty but to her horror, she saw total chaos. Drawers and cupboards had been emptied and the contents tipped all over the floor. She gasped and rushed inside.

The door was unlocked. She grabbed Gran's old rolling-pin and went into the other rooms. The sitting-room was also a mess and she felt tears of anger coursing down her cheeks. How could anyone do this to her? After the last visit from thieves, she thought she was safe, and, she would never have left the door open, nor did she leave the key outside any more.

She ran upstairs, ready to hit anyone over the head with the rolling-pin. There was no-one. She looked round the bedrooms and even under the beds. Nothing. Then, as she left the bathroom, she trod on something soft. She stifled a scream as she saw the body of a rat lying on the step. She did not believe that it could have simply died there. Someone had viciously left it there for her to find. Half sobbing, she ran downstairs and picked up the phone. It was dead.

'Not again,' she cursed.

She found her bag and dialled on her mobile. She sat among the chaos, not even attempting to tidy up. The police had told her to leave things as they were. As far as she could see, there was nothing missing. It was a horrible, pointless attack on her. Someone was making it quite obvious that she was not welcome. But why? Who would do such a thing? Her grandparents had lived here for years. For most of her young life, so had she. It was a complete mystery.

'Damn you,' she said aloud. 'Damn you.'

There were no tears this time, just fury. She felt angrier than she had ever felt in her life. If someone was trying to make her leave and give up on her plans, they could stop right now. She would show them. She would install a burglar alarm, add locks and bars to every door and window, whatever it took. There was no way she was leaving this place, unless it was on her terms.

The police officer who came was the same one who had attended on her arrival. He was very sympathetic but could offer little hope of discovering the culprits.

'I'd have said it was kids,' he suggested, 'but in light of the previous attack on the property, it looks as if someone is trying to make you feel unwelcome here.'

'I simply don't understand it. Who could hate me so much?'

'I doubt it's personal. Much more likely someone trying to buy the land or business.'

'Someone told me that Gramps was thinking of giving up. Maybe there was someone trying to buy him out.'

Jess sat silent for a moment. The someone had been Drew. Suppose he was the person trying to get rid of her. He'd already suggested she should move out of the cottage and stay in his place. Did he have a hidden agenda? She'd thought he was too good to be true.

'Have you thought of something, miss?' the policeman asked. 'You look thoughtful enough.'

'Not really. Well, I'm not sure. Just my imagination running riot.'

'Right then. I'll be on my way. Give us a call if you think of anything else that might help.'

'Thanks, I will. Oh, and thanks for the leaflets. I shall certainly put in an alarm system.'

She watched him leave and glanced

at her watch. Drew would be here in a few minutes and she wasn't changed or showered or anything, and the house was a total shambles.

She couldn't contemplate going out for an evening's pleasure, if that's what it turned out to be. She wasn't even sure she wanted to face Drew. She picked up her mobile and dialled his number. An answering machine picked up the call. She was too late. He'd left home already. She heard his car stop and tried to pull herself together. She opened the door and waited as he walked up the path. He was carrying a box.

'You haven't brought breakfast again, have you?' she tried to joke.

Somehow, she must get through the next five minutes without letting her worrying suspicions show.

'Should I have done?' he asked, a quizzical look on his face.

'Of course not,' Jess said, blushing as she realised the implication of her words.

'I've got something I thought you'd be pleased to see.'

He handed her the box and followed her into the cottage.

'Good grief. What's happened here? Is this a drastic spring-cleaning routine or what?'

'Another break-in, I'm afraid. Nothing appears to be missing. Sheer vandalism, the police suggested.'

'But that's ridiculous! It's so pointless!'

'Isn't all vandalism pointless?' Jess asked coldly.

'Unless . . . unless it's someone trying to make you leave.'

'I came to that conclusion myself.'

'But who would go to these lengths?'

'I can't say. Any ideas?'

'I'll give it some thought. Look, you probably don't feel like leaving the place now. Why don't I go and find us a takeaway? Look in your box. I hope you'll be pleased. Won't be long.'

He turned and went out of the door

again, leaving Jess standing open-mouthed at his audacity. How could he be so cool about this, unless it really wasn't his responsibility? Whatever would his motivation be? She was under no illusions that he had romantic designs in mind. No-one would go to such lengths. In any case, it would be pointless. Whatever or whoever it was, they would not succeed.

She straightened one of the tables and put the box on top of it. Wrapped in newspaper inside the box was Gran's silver tea service. Drew must have bought it for her. She felt a lump in her throat as she fingered the shining metal, remembering so well the feel of it. She and Emily had cleaned it so many times in their young lives.

Wearily, Jess began to tidy up the worst of the mess. She put some plates to warm ready for the meal Drew was collecting. She set the silver on the sideboard and smiled. It was symbolic. It was the beginning of getting every-thing put right. In her heart, she knew

Drew could never have done such a terrible thing as to trash her home. All the same, she would need to be cautious with him. Her feelings were likely to get out of control unless she kept a firm hold on herself.

Her mobile phone rang. Probably Drew to ask if she liked something or other.

'Jess? I need to talk.'

'Em? I suppose that's why you phoned,' she said lightly.

'I'm not in a joking mood. Jess, I'm in terrible trouble.'

Her sister burst into tears and could hardly speak.

'Whatever's the matter? Emily, stop crying and tell me, for goodness' sake,' she said sharply, trying to stop the outburst.

'I'm desperate.'

'You're not making any sense. Why don't you blow your nose and start at the beginning?'

'Oh, Jess, Michael's left me.'

'Who's Michael?'

'Only the most wonderful man in the entire universe. We were getting married and everything.'

'Oh, I see.'

Jess was accustomed to Emily's excesses and assumed this was another one of the string of admirers Emily always seemed to acquire.

'Maybe it's a good job you found out what Michael's really like before you married him,' Jess said sensibly.

'He's got a wife already, but they don't get on. He said he was leaving her and that we were going to get married. Now everything's gone wrong. I don't know what to do. I've packed in my job and everything. We were going to America.'

Her voice failed as a new bout of sobs took over.

'Emily, I'd have thought you were much too streetwise to fall for that one.'

It got worse, Jess thought. Crazy, flighty Emily.

'But he's different. Look, I'm broke now. Can you lend me some money?

After all, you got the lot from our grandparents, didn't you?'

'There's no money, Em. In fact, everything is rather grim. If I didn't have some of my own savings, I wouldn't even have a crop to plant, and there have been quite a few problems.'

'You're so selfish, Jess. Think about me for a change. My life is in tatters. At least you've got a roof over your head.'

'Only just,' Jess replied grimly.

'Please, Jess. I don't want to beg but I'm desperate. Why not just give up and sell the rotting heap? You might get a decent price. Who knows?'

They talked a while longer, but suddenly Emily lost her temper and put the phone down. Jess was deeply upset and wondering what on earth she could do or say to help resolve things. Emily was always the same. She lived up to the hilt and didn't even know what savings were. Jess was still gazing at the phone when Drew returned.

'Hope you like Indian,' he said cheerfully. 'And I've brought some wine as well. Hope you've got some glasses. I didn't think to bring any. Well, what did you think of your surprise?'

'What?' Jess said absently.

'Tea service. I thought you'd be just the tiniest bit grateful. It is the right one, isn't it?'

'I'm sorry. Yes, Drew. It's lovely. Thank you, but I can't let you spend all that money. I must pay you back, of course.'

Goodness, she was thinking. How can I pay out any money? She had set aside the minimum she needed for the new season's planting and now she had to fork out for a burglar alarm as well.

'It's a gift,' he insisted. 'Now, have you got plates and cutlery? We need to eat this before it gets cold.'

'Drew, do you want to buy this place?'

'Buy Tamarisk Cottage? I thought you were fighting like mad to keep it?'

'I am, of course, but I just wondered, purely hypothetically, would you be interested in buying it?'

'I suppose I could. I hadn't really thought about it. If it would help you . . . '

'That isn't what I meant. I wondered if your business has something to do with property.'

'Why worry your pretty head about what I do? I'm successful. That's the most important thing.'

Jess glared at him. How dare he be so patronising? Pretty head, for goodness' sake. Who did he think she was? Who did he think he was, come to that?

'Drew, I am grateful for your generosity, and your help, but I am a fully adult person in my own right, not some toy you can pick up to play with when the mood takes you. The reason I was asking if you wanted to buy the property was because I believe that someone is deliberately setting out to make me feel unwelcome, and, well . . . '

'You just happened to wonder if it was me? Well, thanks a bunch. I've gone out of my way to make you feel welcome. I like you. I remember you from childhood days. I'd hardly want to turn you out when you've just arrived.'

His eyes glinted dangerously. Jess realised immediately the foolishness of tackling him the way she had. Even if he did want to buy the place, he was hardly likely to employ such underhand tactics and he certainly wasn't about to tell her if he did have plans.

'Drew, I'm sorry, really sorry. My mouth ran away with itself once more.'

'You always were a little feisty. I'm sorry, too. I didn't mean to be patronising. I really want to help. You're very brave, trying to get this wreck of a business up and running again.'

'You say brave but I think you mean foolhardy, mad, ridiculous.'

He looked at her and made no comment. After the silence, he moved toward the table.

'If we are going to eat anything, I suggest we stop this silly argument right now. Come on, Jess. Let's get some food inside us. Things never look quite so bleak on a full stomach.'

Jess had lost her appetite and suddenly felt incredibly weary. She actually wished he would leave and let her get to bed.

'You know,' she said after several minutes of pushing food around her plate, 'this business only makes me even more determined to make a success of it all. I owe it to my grandparents. It meant everything to them and they were more than parents to us, Emily and me.'

'Oh, yes, of course. Your sister, Emily. How is she faring these days?'

With a jolt, Jess realised that she hadn't given a further thought to Emily and whatever her latest catastrophe might bring.

'OK. Well, as OK as she ever is. My sister is never known for making life easy. She has a new drama every fortnight and probably as many new men as well.'

Jess bit her lip after she had spoken. She hadn't meant to let her private thoughts show and certainly not to say something so disloyal to someone who was after all, virtually a stranger.

'I see. Always was a bit unruly, if I remember correctly. Always ready to take chances.'

'And I was the safe, reliable one. Boring, in other words.'

He smiled at her, his remarkable eyes turning a soft, smoky grey. He really was most attractive, she speculated.

'Nothing wrong with being reliable, and I'd hardly say that someone about to embark on a very difficult, uncertain business, was altogether boring. No, Jess, I think you're one gutsy lady. I wish you luck. Now, perhaps you'd like a hand to get this place tidied up a bit? I take it the police have seen all they want?'

She nodded and began to stack the plates. She realised how little she'd eaten and apologised to Drew. He brushed it aside and began to roll his sleeves up. They chatted briefly as they worked. Straightening things and picking up some of the broken remains of her possessions made a difference and soon the room began to look neat again.

'Nobody, but nobody is going to make me move from here, not until I decide that it's the right thing for me to do.'

Jess stood firm, looking round the familiar room that was slowly beginning to be her home.

'Good for you,' Drew said quietly, his words contradicting the strange look in his eyes.

Jess said nothing but pondered over the man's sudden involvement in her life. He always seemed to be where she was. Always seemed to turn up at the most opportune moments.

'I'm sorry, Drew, but I'm exhausted. I must get some sleep. I have to make an early start tomorrow.'

'I'll go then. Please, Jess, do consider my suggestion. Move down to the hotel for a while, just until you can get yourself sorted out. Forget your attempts to try to make a living from this heap. You're simply not suited to this sort of life. Cut your losses.'

'How dare you, Drew Rogers? How dare you try to tell me what to do? Two weeks ago I had no idea of who you even were. I'd never given you a thought since I was trying to get you out of my life for tormenting me as a child. I'm grateful for all your help and for the silver you kindly returned to me. I will pay you back, I promise. But now, I'd like you to leave me alone. Whatever I decide in the long term, it will be my decision when I'm good and ready.'

'I think that's my cue to leave,' he snapped, grey eyes glinting like steel again. 'Phone me if you feel you'd like to. I won't bother you again.'

He left the cottage, slamming the door somewhat harder than necessary. Jess could hear him stamping up the path and knew she had probably seen the last of him, at least for some while. She sat in front of the fire and watched the last remains of the wood as it burned away. She felt very alone and almost regretted sending away the one friend she had in the area.

Her mind drifted towards her sister. What sort of mess had Emily landed in this time? She reached for the phone and pressed Emily's number. It was the answering machine so she left a brief message, asking for her to call back as soon as possible. Maybe she ought to consider selling up. It may not fetch much of a price, this old farm, but it would probably be enough for a substantial deposit on somewhere else. She could give Em a share, too, to help out with the current crisis at the very least.

'I'm sorry, Gramps,' she whispered. 'I promised I would do my best but it really is very hard.'

She sat listening to the faint crackle of the fire and the wind blowing outside. Childhood days rushed to fill her mind. She recalled the days when Gran had struggled in with fresh wood to keep the fire going and to warm

Gramps' cold feet when he came in. Then there was the fun they'd had as children, making jam from the jars of blackberries gathered from prickly hedgerows. She smiled. If ever she had children of her own, they must experience some of these old country occupations. Old values and the old ways of a simple life should never be entirely forgotten. With a new feeling of resolve, she climbed the narrow stairs and went into her old bedroom. This was where she should be, where she wanted to be. Tomorrow, she would set to and get that field ploughed, whatever it took.

4

Jess awoke early, feeling surprisingly refreshed. The problems of the previous day had receded to some extent and she felt ready to tackle whatever the day held, with energy and enthusiasm. She ate a large bowl of porridge, drank several cups of coffee and went out into the crisp, cold day. The sun was shining though there was a cold wind blowing.

She pulled her hat down over her ears and zipped up the old anorak, striding along the rough path to the shed where the tractor was kept. Her determination paid off. The old machine croaked into life and soon, she was hauling the plough back and forth across the field. She had been helping with this task for as long as she could remember. The smell of freshly-turned ground sent her mind back to childhood when she and Emily had taken turns to ride on the tractor beside Gramps, squealing with laughter as they turned corners and could see the flocks of sea birds pecking at the ground.

The smell of the sea wafted up to her and she knew she was where she most wanted to be. She smiled as she looked at the neat furrows behind her. Gramps would have been proud of her. By early afternoon, the job was finished. She felt her stomach rumbling with hunger and drove the tractor back to the shed, totally satisfied with her morning's work.

In the kitchen, Jess rummaged in the cupboard to find something to eat. She opened a can of soup and put some frozen bread rolls into the warm oven. There was a small piece of cheese to go with the rest, though that would almost empty the fridge completely. She needed to go shopping again. Gran had never run out of everything the way she seemed to.

She made a list while she ate her

meal. She would do a supermarket run and really stock up. The future seemed suddenly brighter. She sang as she drove the few miles to Penzance. Though there was a small shop in the village, she discounted this in favour of the stores in the town where she could buy larger packets of things she used a lot.

Once more she wandered down the road where the antique shops were and looked in the windows to see if there were any more of her stolen possessions in the windows. There was nothing. As she looked into one shop, she caught sight of Drew talking to the proprietor. She was sure he'd seen her as she turned and walked away quickly. She glanced behind her but if he had seen her, he wasn't following. Strangely, she felt no surprise. She was getting used to seeing him wherever she went. What she was not used to, was the sudden pounding her heart seemed to take on.

'Must be getting the equivalent of a

teenage crush,' she told herself, laughing. 'So unlike Jess Farley.'

Once the serious shopping was out of the way, Jess began her drive back home. The nights were drawing in and it was already getting dark. Her lights picked out a sign along the road **Jack Russell Puppies For Sale. Ready now.**

'That's just what I need,' she muttered, 'a dog. It would be a companion and also help deter any yobs who think they'll make themselves at home in Tamarisk Cottage.'

Impulsively, she stopped the car and went up the path to the house with the sign. She knocked at the door. Immediately, a chorus of yapping and more adult dog barking filled her ears.

'Get out of the way,' a female voice called out.

Jess smiled. How could anyone be lonely with a houseful of dogs? The door opened and a flustered-looking woman peered out.

'Yes?' she asked. 'How can I help?'

'I'm thinking of getting a pup and thought I'd like to see what you have.'

'Come in, dear. You'll have to excuse the mess. The kids have just got in after their football practice and I'm trying to get the meal ready.'

'I can always come back another time,' Jess said uncomfortably. 'I mean, it was only on impulse that I stopped.'

'It's rarely any different here, so you may as well come in now.'

The woman was cheerfully accepting of her untidy home. Two puppies leaped on her feet the moment Jess stepped into the living-room. They settled themselves to chew the laces of her trainers with absolute contentment.

'Get off, you two,' the woman said, waving her hands at them. 'I'm sorry. They're absolute menaces. Oh, dear, I shouldn't say that, should I? Put you right off them.'

Jess leaned down to pick up one of the pups. They were mostly white with brown and black markings.

'They're practically identical, aren't

87

they?' she remarked. 'Are they boys or girls?'

Both girls, bitches, she was told. How on earth could anyone choose between two such identical dogs? They were totally captivating and Jess fell in love instantly.

'How much for the pair?'

'Oh, my dear, do you know what you're taking on? Two puppies at the same time?'

'At least I can train them together, and they'll be company for each other. Maybe they'll settle better.'

'Twice the puppy teeth to chew everything and twice the puddles. Believe me, I know it only too well.'

But Jess was adamant, both or neither. They talked money and agreed a discounted price for the two.

'I'll have to collect them another time. I haven't got anything ready yet.'

She drove the rest of the way home, her mind a mixture of pleasure and worry about her impulse. How would she cope with all the work she had to do and two small dogs to train? Several times during the evening, she almost picked up the phone to cancel the deal but she didn't.

Just as she was going to bed, the phone rang. She gave a start. It must be Emily. She had meant to call her back and had quite forgotten.

'Jess?' a trembling voice said when she picked up the phone. 'It's Em.'

'Hi. How are you? Sorry, I meant to call back but I've been busy.'

'It's OK. I did put the phone down on you, last night. Sorry. Jess, I'm really in trouble this time, serious trouble. Can I come down and stay for a bit, until I decide what to do?'

' 'Course you can. It's a bit primitive here but you must remember what it's like. When do you plan to arrive?'

'Sometime next week, if that's OK. I'll let you know nearer the time.'

'What's wrong, Em?'

'I'll tell you everything when I see you. 'Bye for now.'

Jess frowned. It had to be something

fairly major for this sort of behaviour. If Emily needed help, she would always be there for her but all the same she had a great deal of work to do. The house wasn't really in any state to have guests and there was all the planting to be done. If it was delayed any longer, she would be too late for the spring crop. There was also the matter of two puppies she had agreed to buy.

Wearily, she climbed the stairs and crawled into her welcome bed. It had been a long day. She dreamed of Drew and woke suddenly, half expecting him to be downstairs. She put the light on. Four o'clock. She cursed and turned over to go back to sleep, but it was no good. She was awake and already planning things that needed doing. She pulled a sweater over her pyjamas and put on her cosy slippers.

She put the kettle on the warm range and spooned coffee powder into a mug. She rummaged in Gramps' old filing cabinet and pulled out dog-eared bulb catalogues. She needed to get the bulbs delivered as soon as possible and into the ground. She knew that she was asking the impossible in some ways as orders usually had to be in very much earlier than this. She would be lucky to get anything, let alone first-quality bulbs. She noted down numbers and references and hoped that when she phoned later that morning, she would get a sympathetic ear when she explained.

Things seemed to be falling into place, she discovered later that day. One of Gramps' suppliers had kept back a quantity of bulbs for the old man. They had decided to plant them themselves, if he didn't contact them soon. When she explained what had happened and how she was planning to try and run the farm herself, they couldn't have been nicer.

'Your grandfather was so proud of you. He always said you'd be the one to make the daffodils work. Now, we can't get the bulbs to you today but with luck and a following wind, they'll be with you Thursday morning. How's that?'

'Wonderful,' Jess whispered, her emotions running high with gratitude and relief.

The supplier had given her a good deal of information about planting, quantities and the care, saving her many hours of checking through Gramps' old reference books and files. Thank goodness the vandals and burglars hadn't found the records and destroyed all of them as well. Gran may have complained about the dirty, old filing cabinet filling the cupboard under the stairs, but at least it had been spared the devastation the rest of the place had suffered.

Now, she would spend the entire day clearing up the rubbish from the daffodil field and make sure it was quite ready for its crop to be planted. If there was time later, she would go and buy the basic necessities for her two new little friends. It would be best if she could get the bulbs planted before their arrival, however, and she made a note to call the breeder later in the day and postpone collecting them for a few days.

Life was almost good, she decided. If it wasn't for her silly row with Drew and whatever trouble Emily had got into, the future would be something to approach with total optimism. Even Drew's name had an effect on her. Maybe she should apologise for her unreasonable behaviour. She was certain his intentions were for her own good and she had merely been objecting to the way he seemed to want to organise her life. He couldn't really be responsible for any of the break-ins or other problems she had encountered, could he? She would call him later, in the evening perhaps. She might even make a peace offering of a meal.

Apart from a brief stop for lunch, Jess worked all day. She collected bits of wood and the unbroken weeds from the field and made a heap near the tractor shed. She could have a bonfire later, she decided. Tomorrow, the back-breaking task of planting bulbs would fill her day. It would take many hours to plant the entire field so she'd decided to plant a reduced crop for this year. The important thing was to have some sort of product to sell at the end, if only to make the name known once more. In future years, she would be better organised.

'Jess,' she heard a voice call.

She rose wearily from her bent position, barely able to straighten after her exhausting day. She couldn't see anyone at first but then noticed the familiar car parked near the field gate.

'Jess? I came to apologise,' Drew called. 'Am I forgiven yet? I promise not to try to tell you what to do, ever again.'

'Drew,' she called back in some surprise. 'Hi. I was going to phone you this evening and try to make some sort of peace offering. I was very rude. I s'pose it's all proving a bit much.'

They stood together near the shed and surveyed the results of her efforts.

'I can't believe you've managed all this in so short a time. You're quite amazing. All on your own?'

' 'Course,' she said, pleased by his praise. 'I told you I was tougher than I look.'

'I wondered if you'd like to eat out somewhere. I only managed a takeaway last time I offered. Only if you haven't any other plans, of course.'

'I was planning to collapse into a hot bath and find something in the freezer.'

'Another time maybe?'

'I could always find two somethings from the freezer, as a gesture of goodwill,' she offered.

'Sounds good to me. I'll bring some wine. Sevenish suit you?'

'Fine. Gives me time to make some calls and see about organising my puppies.'

'What puppies?' he asked.

'I'm getting two pups, guard dogs, sort of.'

'German Shepherds? Rottweilers?'

'Jack Russells. Don't want to inflict

too much damage on any intruders.'

'Think I might feel safer with a Shepherd,' he said ruefully. 'Jackies snap and bark a lot. One never knows where one is with small dogs.'

She glared warningly. He grinned and held up a hand in surrender.

'OK. Just allow me to have some opinions of my own, even if you don't agree. I'll see you later. Enjoy your bath.'

He left her standing amidst her vast open space. She closed her eyes and could see rows of waving daffodils in her mind's eye. The chilly wind reminded her that there was a long way to go before her vision could be realised.

5

By the end of the evening, Drew and Jessica seemed to have repaired a few bridges and the mood between them was good. Jess finally admitted to herself that she definitely had feelings for this man, powerful feelings that could lead her into difficulties if she allowed him any suspicion of them. She would have to be very careful to keep things simple and on a purely friendly level. He was not the sort of man to whom one could dictate terms, not on an emotional level.

All the same, thinking of him gave her a warm, happy feeling inside and she knew that was worth a great deal. She sensed he would always want more. He would expect all sorts of commitment should things progress. No way could she allow that to happen. For now, they could be good friends and hopefully, things could stay that way indefinitely.

'Did I tell you that my sister, Emily, is coming down next week? Some new crisis in her life. She seems to flit from one crisis to the next so I never take anything too seriously.'

'Quite a looker, if I remember correctly. All big blue eyes and long blonde curls.'

'You've got it.' Jess laughed. 'Maybe not quite so curly these days, but the eyes are still there and she's still blonde.'

'I'll look forward to having two ladies to escort to dinner one evening then. We may even make it to my favourite restaurant. I do assure you they can cook in Cornwall, despite your apparent wish to refuse to eat out.'

He held up a hand before she could speak.

'It's OK. I was only teasing. Well, I'd better get on my way. I, too, have an early start tomorrow, a trip to Bristol. Business, of course.'

'Think I'd almost prefer to plant daffodil bulbs,' Jess said cheerfully.

'No accounting for taste.' Drew said grinning. 'At least I don't have to dig endless mud off my boots at the end of the day. See you soon. I'm glad we made it up. I think I could be very fond of you, Jess, very fond, indeed.'

Jess grinned, hoping he was unaware of her trembling frame. She knew that if he tried to kiss her again, she would find it very hard to stop him, let alone stop herself from responding to him.

'Just as well,' she said lightly. 'I shall be troubling you for all sorts of help no doubt. I think I'm beginning to perfect my damsel in distress routine.'

He stared at her for a moment but luckily, made no further comment.

' 'Night Jess,' he said lightly, as he pushed the door open.

' 'Night,' Jess replied, torn between wanting him to kiss her and knowing that she should not give away how she really felt.

Men like Drew Rogers did not fall in

love, least of all with a poverty-stricken idiot trying to make the impossible happen. As he drove off, she remembered that she had not phoned the dog lady. She cursed, knowing it was much too late to call now. It would be her first job tomorrow, she promised herself. She looked round the cosy room. It only needed two puppies to scamper around to make it seem like a real home. She really would have to give thought to where they would sleep and stay during the days she wasn't taking them out with her.

The van with the daffodil bulbs arrived soon after nine. She looked at the mountain of sacks, each containing over one hundred bulbs and practically ordered them to be taken away. It was a task and a half to plant them all, especially single-handed. She wished there was someone she could ask to help. Apart from Drew, she seemed to know no-one at all. She giggled, thinking of the immaculate man stooping over the muddy earth planting bulbs. All the same, he might know of someone she could employ. Another pair of hands would make all the difference.

She began to haul the heavy sacks on to the tractor's low trailer. At least she could drive them to where she needed them. She began the backbreaking chore and worked through till lunch time, almost unable to straighten up when she came to the end of a row. She would have to get someone to help her, whatever pride she might have to swallow when asking for it.

To Jess's amazement, soon after two o'clock, Drew arrived wearing jeans and Wellington boots and accompanied by two young men who evidently did odd jobs for him. She then drove the tractor along the rows and Drew sat on the trailer dropping off bulbs which the two planted. They worked until daylight had almost gone when wearily, she put the tractor back in the shed. The small pile of sacks of bulbs that remained could easily be planted by the following lunch time.

She invited her helpers into the cottage and produced beers for them all to drink and some crisps. Her mind raced through thoughts of what there might be to eat in her small stock cupboard, but once more, Drew came to the rescue by suggesting he fetched fish and chips for everyone. Despite near exhaustion, they spent a happy evening, laughing and chatting about the farm, the village and the general shortage of work.

'I'd like to be able to offer you jobs but I'm afraid I just can't afford more than casual labour.'

'Any time you need us,' one of the young men told her, 'just ask. We keep busy round the farms and doing odd carpentry jobs. We manage,' he concluded.

'I must give you something for your time this afternoon. I'm so grateful for your help.'

'It's all right,' the younger one told her. 'We was on Mr Roger's time today.

Sort it with him.'

'Yer,' the other added. 'Ta for the fish and chips and beers. Think we'd better be off now though. Things to do.'

'Er . . . right. Thanks again. I'll square it with Drew then.'

She saw them out and returned to the cosy sitting-room, wondering how on earth she was actually going to sort the financial matters with Drew.

'I really am grateful to you,' she began.

'Delighted I could help, and don't even think about paying. I have those two on a weekly basis anyhow, and didn't actually have anything that needed doing. Couldn't have been a better time to ask. It goes as business expenses as well.'

'Well,' Jess replied, 'it's most kind of you and I am truly grateful. Thank you again.'

She felt slightly troubled by the situation but she didn't want it to become another independence issue.

'If you don't mind, I think I should

leave now. My limbs are screaming out for a long, hot bath and I'm sure yours are, too. Sure you'll manage the rest tomorrow?' Drew asked.

'Quite sure, thanks. Only a few left to do and then I shall go and sort out my new pups.'

'You don't give yourself much of a break, do you?'

'I'm fine. Thanks again.'

'Don't keep thanking me. I wouldn't do anything unless I wanted to. See you soon,' he said, as he opened the door.

The smell of the sea and the freshly-turned earth mingled on the cold night air. The moon was rising, illuminating the landscape all around.

'Silver stripes across the sea,' Jess remarked.

Drew turned, came back towards her and planted a kiss firmly on her mouth. She shivered, partly from the cold air and partly because he was acting in the only way she could have wanted. Curse the man. Why did he have this effect on her? He was only being friendly after all so why should she even try to make it into anything more? Silently, he turned back to his waiting car and she watched as his tail lights disappeared down the hill.

She went back into the cottage and closed the door firmly. Lying in her hot bath, she heard the phone ringing. She cursed gently but was too weary and too warm in the bath to rush out to answer it. She heard the answering machine click on and a female voice speaking. Must be Em, she concluded, and made a silent promise to call her back later.

'Jess, where are you? I really need to talk. Call me.'

The message sounded urgent but then, that was Em. Everything in her life was always urgent.

'Em? What's up?' she asked when she dialled the number, a little later.

'I can't begin to tell you on the phone. I'm coming down tomorrow, if that's OK. I've booked a ticket. Meet me at Penzance, will you?'

'Couldn't you leave it another day? I'm up to my eyes tomorrow. Won't have time to get your room ready or anything.'

'I'll sleep on the couch. You can't stop me from coming down. Please, Jess. It's really important.'

'What on earth is it? If it's another of your major crises that turns into nothing . . .'

'Oh, not this one. Sorry, Jess, have to go. Must do my packing. I'll call when the train's near. 'Bye.'

'Em, really.'

But the line was dead. There was nothing else she could do or say. With a deep sigh, she went upstairs to the room Em had always had as a child. It was a shambles. Jess hauled the mattress downstairs to air it overnight, in front of the range. She stuffed the odd bits of junk into plastic bags and put them in the room once shared by her grandparents. Somehow, it had never seemed right to occupy it herself. Emily's room looked sparse and unwelcoming. She would have to spend precious time cleaning it and finding bits of furniture to put in there. At least Em was only coming for a short stay and by train as well, so she wouldn't be bringing much luggage.

Whatever the problem was, it would be good to see her sister. They hadn't spent time together for ages. Again she remembered the puppies she was supposed to be collecting. It was once more too late to phone the breeder. She must do it in the morning or she would think Jess had changed her mind. It might have been a bit rash in the circumstances, she thought, but she had promised to buy them and she'd even paid a small deposit. Her weary body would not let her do more and she tumbled into bed, falling asleep immediately.

She awoke suddenly, aware of a light coming into the room. She never drew the curtains as there was no-one to overlook her and she enjoyed the morning sun waking her, but this was most definitely not the sun. It was still dark, except for the red, flickering light coming from across the field.

She leaped out of bed and rushed to the window. She could see a blaze, in the direction of the shed. She pulled clothes on quickly, over the top of her pyjamas and grabbing wellies at the door, rushed over to the shed. The blaze had well and truly taken hold and the old wooden building was well alight. The tractor wasn't yet burning and she put her arms over her head and rushed in, heedless of the danger she was in. She tried to start it. The heat was intense and she felt her face getting hot. She tried again, desperate to rescue the old machine.

It coughed into life and she put it in gear and drove out of the shed, causing the burning wall to collapse behind her. Shaking with relief and shock, she stopped the machine and almost fell off it. There was nothing she could do about the rest of the shed, apart from watch it burn. The precious remaining bulbs were in there, too, lost, destroyed. Thank goodness she had got the bulk of the stock planted.

She stood watching, helpless and distraught. How on earth could the fire have started and got hold so quickly? It wasn't as if the shed was dry even. The rain over the past few weeks must have soaked it through. As her thoughts raced, she became aware of the sounds of a fire engine approaching. How on earth had they known? They must have been alerted some time ago to have got here so quickly. There wasn't much they could do at this stage, she thought.

They drove in through the field gate and straight across the land she'd already planted. She bit her lip.

'It's too late, I'm afraid,' Jess mumbled to a fireman who ran over to her.

'Are you all right?' he asked anxiously. 'Good job the tractor wasn't in there,' he added, spotting the old machine standing some way off.

'It was. I drove it out,' Jess told him,

feeling near to tears.

'You took a risk. You shouldn't have risked your life over that ancient bit of machinery.'

'I couldn't just let it burn. It's the only thing I've got to work the ground. How did you know about the fire? Who called you?'

'Someone out at sea. Local fisherman. He knew the set-up here and called us on his radio. Thought it was something we needed to attend.'

The fire crew was still pulling out hoses and sprayed water from the tender over the fire. There wasn't much left to quench. The long shed, also used for packing flowers in the season, was quite destroyed, along with the remaining bulbs.

'We'll need to try and find out how it started. Any ideas? What was stored in there? Petrol? Old paint?'

'Nothing like that. The diesel is kept right away from the shed. It's in a storage tank over at the edge of the field, but that's empty now anyhow. I was going to order some tomorrow. Apart from that, the only stuff in the shed was old packing boxes and the rest of the bulbs I was planning to plant tomorrow.'

One of the other men called to the chief. He excused himself and went to see what his colleague had found. Jess stood where she was, hearing the male voices but unaware of what they were saying. At last, one of them came over to her.

'We're pretty sure the fire was started deliberately. There's a strong smell of petrol and I do mean petrol, not the diesel the tractor uses. Is there anyone you can think of who might have a grudge? Wants to put you out of business?'

'Of course not. Well, there is obviously someone who wanted me to feel unwelcome.'

She told him briefly about the break-ins.

'We'll have to call the police. Meantime, I suggest you go back in the warm and we'll be across in a while to sort a few details. I'll radio for the police. You could occupy yourself with a kettle,' he added with a grin.

Jess trudged back to the cottage. Who on earth would have gone to these lengths to destroy her property? Someone either had a long-held grudge or there was some other motive behind it all. She remembered the strange man she had seen during her first days here. He'd seemed to be measuring or something. Could it be that a developer was after the land? But would anyone go to these lengths to make her sell up? If there was enough money involved, who could tell? Prime sites like this one did not often come up for sale.

Unwillingly, her mind turned back to Drew, but he couldn't be connected with this in any way. After all, he had spent a long afternoon helping her and even provided two workers to help. She felt guilty about the very thought but then, she had seen that man at Drew's place one day. There was some connection between them. He had also suggested she should give up her battle and let the place go. Well, he didn't know the Farley determination. This latest set-back made it even more important to her that she should succeed.

'They won't knock us back, Gramps. I promise you.'

After pouring endless cups of tea for the assorted fire crew and policemen, Jess felt as if running a café would be easy. It was almost dawn and already too late to contemplate more sleep. She felt drained, exhausted, and Emily was coming later in the day. Nothing was ready for her sister's arrival and now Jess had to decide if she should try to get more bulbs to plant or settle for what was already in the ground. She also realised that many of them were probably destroyed after the wheels of the fire engine and all the boots trampling everywhere.

'Right, love, we'll be getting on our way,' the chief fireman told her. 'The police will take your statement and advise you of the case number and all for your insurance. You should be able to get something back for the damage and loss of potential earnings.'

She saw them all off, with a sense of relief. If the insurance covered the loss, she might just get away without planting more bulbs. She didn't think she could have faced another day in the field even if she could get more daffodils to plant. She climbed the stairs feeling more like bedtime than morning and showered and dressed. She heard a car stop outside and sighed. It was going to be one of those days.

'Hi!' a male voice called. 'It's Drew. You there?'

'Just coming,' she called down. 'Put the kettle on, why don't you.'

She heard the crashing sounds of the kettle and came down to find Drew looking in the fridge.

'I thought I'd cook you some breakfast but there seems to be nothing much in. I could scramble an egg if you like.'

'I've been up since . . . oh, I don't know. I'd throw up if I had to eat.'

'I was so sorry to hear the latest drama. How awful for you. Much damage?'

'The shed's completely gone. I managed to save the tractor.'

'So I heard. You should have left it. The insurance would probably have bought you another.'

'I didn't think at the time. Anyhow, how do you know so much?'

'Talk of the village. Mrs Jamieson was full of it. Rotten luck.'

'That's as may be, but I don't think luck came into it. They seem to think it was deliberate.'

She spoke calmly, much more so than she felt. She looked at him carefully as she spoke but his eyes looked straight back at hers. If he had anything to do with it, it certainly didn't show.

'Look, thanks for coming round but

I have masses to do. My sister, bless her, has decided she can't wait to see me any longer. She's coming today and I haven't got anything ready for her. In fact I think I have to go out and buy some things. I've been managing on what I'd got for just me but with two of us, it will be difficult. And I have to speak to the police, fire investigators and anyone else who fancies seeing me. I might even be suspect number one. You know the sort of thing — insurance fraud and compensation. I really think the someone trying to drive me out might just be succeeding.'

She couldn't help but notice a flicker of interest or something similar cross Drew's face. She wondered yet again if he was capable of such dreadful deeds. Of course he couldn't be. All the same, it was difficult to know. He put comforting arms round her and she snuggled against him.

'Poor little Jess. It's been a rotten time for you. Don't forget I'm here for you. Please let me help you. Forget that stubborn pride of yours and accept what I can offer.'

'Thank you, Drew, but I'll be OK, honest.'

She felt guilty about her earlier thoughts.

It was around one thirty when her mobile rang. Emily was nearing the station and wanted collecting. Jess quickly locked the door and set off for Penzance. She stopped outside the station and saw her sister, looking pale and unwell and surrounded by a heap of luggage.

'Lovely to see you, Em,' she called as she ran across the road. 'Good gracious! However much luggage have you brought?'

'The rest's being sent by carrier. It's cheaper that way. Oh, Jess.'

She flung herself into her older sister's arms and sobbed.

'Hey, come on. This isn't like you. Let's get the stuff to the car, as much of it as we can. You must have needed half a dozen porters for this lot.'

Jess began to pick up the assortment of packages and boxes, leaving the two large cases to her sister. She dropped it by the car and turned to help with the rest. Em was still standing on the pavement's edge. Jess went back and took the cases. Em trailed behind, looking like a dejected puppy. Jess loaded everything into the car and left the door open for her sister.

'Come on then. Let's get the show on the road. I'm afraid things are still pretty basic at the cottage. After the burglaries, I haven't got around to replacing everything and then with the fire . . . oh, but of course you don't know about that.'

Jess waited for her sister to make some comment but she remained silent. It was almost as if she wasn't hearing anything.

'Come on, Em. This silent treatment isn't like you.'

'I can see you're not really interested

in my troubles. You've babbled non-stop since you arrived. I thought you didn't want to know.'

'Get real, Emily. I never know if you are really in trouble or having one of your all-too-frequent dramas. I'll be quiet. I'm listening. Well? Are you going to tell me or not?'

'Wait till we get home. I could do with something hot inside me first.'

Jess gave a sigh. Trust the drama queen to prolong the agony. Chances were it was all a storm in a teacup. They drove on in virtual silence. Jess gave a start when she saw the sign for puppies for sale. She really must get in touch with that lady.

'Here we are. Tamarisk Cottage in all its glory,' Jess announced cheerfully.

'Thanks,' Emily muttered.

She got out of the car and walked up the path, leaving Jess to ferry in all her luggage. Emily leaned down and lifted the corner of the doormat.

'The key's gone,' she announced in a matter-of-fact tone.

'Did you know about that?' Jess asked.

' 'Course I did. Everyone did. Why?'

'I never knew. Did Gran always leave it there?'

'Yes. Anyhow, are you going to let us in?'

Jess reached across her sister and unlocked the door. She began to put the luggage inside, while Emily flopped down in a chair next to the range.

'Put on the kettle and we'll have some coffee,' Jess suggested.

'I don't drink coffee,' Em replied. 'Have you got camomile tea?'

'Since when don't you drink coffee?'

'Since . . . since I was pregnant.'

Jess felt as if the room was spinning.

'Since what?' she demanded.

'Since I was pregnant. Don't tell me off, Jess. I shall burst into tears.'

'You idiot. How on earth did you let that happen?'

On cue, Em's eyes filled with tears.

'I told you I was an idiot. I believed what Michael told me, that we would be married. I thought this was going to be the icing on the cake. How was I to know he would change his mind? Oh, Jess, what am I going to do?'

6

The rest of the afternoon was spent in long discussions about what they might do. Jess was almost at her wits' end.

'At least we have an adequate roof over our heads, and Michael will surely help out with payments for the baby,' she suggested reasonably.

'Never,' Emily almost shouted. 'I'm not taking a penny off that man. I'll manage somehow. I knew you'd always come through for me. Gramps must have left you a decent amount of money. He always did love you best.'

'Emily, that's not true. He only left it to me because he knew I'd try to make a go of the farm, but there was next to no money. It all went on Gran's care. The only money I have is what I saved during the last year's work and a bit more to buy bulbs to plant. After the fire last night, I face a greatly-reduced amount of profit next year plus a lot of expense in replacing the shed and everything. I know there's the insurance but it hardly covers everything.'

'Where are all the vases and stuff?'

It seemed to Jess that Emily hadn't even heard the word fire.

'The bits Gran always had around, and the pictures. Oh, Jess, you haven't sold them?'

' 'Course not. They were all stolen. I told you about the two burglaries. Well, one was mainly vandalism.'

'You told me? I don't remember.'

Jess sighed. It was typical of her sister. She was so wound up in her own affairs that she didn't think about any one else's troubles. They were spared further discussion by a knock at the door.

'Hi,' Drew said coming in with a huge carton. 'I've brought you some spare goodies from the now defunct hotel. They're only stored in the attic so don't think I've given you anything valuable. There are some spare sheets, crockery, things Mrs J. thought would be useful. You must be Emily. Don't suppose you remember me, Drew Rogers. We used to torment each other when we were kids, according to your sister here.'

'Hello,' Emily said more cheerfully than Jess had seen before. 'I do remember you, of course, but Jess didn't mention you were still around. Did you say the hotel is defunct?'

'I did. Gave it up a few years ago after my parents died. Couldn't face the hassle of running it, so decided to make it my home and run my business from there.'

The two were soon chatting away and Jess began to prepare a simple meal. She felt left out of things and slightly cross. Trust Emily to brighten up when a good-looking man came on the scene. She loved her sister dearly but she had always taken everything for granted all her life. She was the pretty one people always felt the need to look after. Even now they were adults, nothing had changed.

With Drew's offerings from the hotel, they were at least able to have clean sheets and there were now plenty of plates and cutlery. He stayed around for most of the rest of the day and left during the evening. Emily's urgent problem had not been mentioned in front of Drew and once alone, Jess brought up the subject again.

'I can't make any plans yet,' Emily informed her. 'I thought I'd come here and chill out for a while and then decide on the long-term future with your help. I wasn't sure what you intended doing with your inheritance. Now I know you're staying on, I might as well stay, too. We can make a go of it together.'

'You really mean that?' Jess asked.

' 'Course. Maybe I can keep house while you work. Do the cooking and everything.'

'You?' Jess exploded. 'You can barely make the toaster work, unless you've been practising.'

'I'll have plenty of time to learn, won't I? We can bring up the baby together, Jess. Just think of it. We managed all right without parents.'

'How can you say that, Em? Gran and Gramps were everything to us.'

'I know, but we shall manage.'

'And what do you think we can live on? I'm never going to make much out of the farm but I have to give it a go for Gramps. I was planning a fairly meagre existence on my own. You'll never manage on the sort of budget I was planning. And have you really thought it through? Babies cost so much money. You'll want the best for your baby and we won't be able to afford it.'

'Drew might help. Maybe I can get a job with him. He must need a secretary.'

'If he needs one, don't you think he'll already have one?'

'Not a London-trained one. I'm very good at office management. I may not be much on the domestic front, but I'm a whiz with computers. That's it. I'll get one here and I can do all the office stuff, and we can have a website. Sell stuff direct.'

'If we ever have anything to sell. Emily, come down to earth. This is Cornwall. We're selling daffodils to a specialised market. We have a very limited amount of customers.'

'See? You're getting used to the idea. You're already saying we. Now, I must get to bed. Which room am I in?'

'Your old one, of course.'

'You've taken Gran's and Gramps' room, have you?'

'No. It didn't seem right, not yet. Besides, rats ate the bed. I haven't got round to a new one yet.'

'Oh, no. How disgusting. You've got rid of them, I hope?'

Jess was tempted to say no, but it wasn't worth the hassle. She sent her sister up to bed, promising cocoa and a proper natter later. Whatever irritation she might be feeling, she put down to her lack of sleep the previous night and her many worries. Emily was just being typical Emily and whatever her short-comings, Jess truly loved her younger sister.

Maybe it was partly her own fault. She had always been there to support Emily, whenever she needed it. Feeling much older than her twenty-six years, she carried two mugs of cocoa up the stairs and sat on her sister's bed. They talked for a long time, until Jess seemed to have convinced Emily that there was very little money available and that they must both work to keep their heads above water.

At eight-thirty the next morning, Drew arrived once more with one of his special breakfasts.

'Just thought you might appreciate some breakfast,' he announced. 'Mrs Jamieson insisted I bring it, so don't take offence.'

Emily staggered down, looking delightfully rumpled and wearing a dressing-gown that barely covered her short nightie.

'Oh,' she exclaimed, 'I didn't expect

visitors so early.'

'I'm not so much a visitor as a butler,' Drew joked. 'If mesdames would care to be seated, I shall serve breakfast.'

Jess frowned slightly. He was taking some things for granted but she didn't want a scene and she actually felt ravenous. Mrs Jamieson's hot, bacon rolls were far too tempting.

'Good job I got over morning sickness, isn't it?' Emily said tucking into her first roll.

'Morning sickness?' Drew echoed. 'I assume that means you're having a baby.'

'Yes, well and truly. Jess is about to become an aunt.'

'Wow,' was Drew's only comment.

'I assume there is no man around, Emily?'

'No. The father doesn't want to know. I don't suppose you're free?' she asked with a grin.

Drew blushed and shook his head. 'Sorry.'

'We'll just have to bring it up with two mothers then, won't we?'

Jess smiled at Drew and shook her head slightly, indicating that they should drop the subject.

'Thanks for the breakfast, Drew. It's very thoughtful of you but we really can't keep accepting your help like this,' she said.

'I enjoy sharing breakfast, so it's my pleasure. Incidentally, I did mean to ask if you've got anything lined up to replace your shed. One of my contacts can supply you with one. I know there's no real hurry till the picking starts but you might like to know where you can get an estimate. Besides, you'll need to keep that poor old tractor under cover for the winter.'

'That would be useful. Thanks again. Seems to me you know someone who can supply just about everything. And you still haven't explained what your business is.'

'Hard to explain. Lots of enterprises

really. Diversification, that's the name of the game.'

'Sounds fascinating,' Emily told him. 'Look, there are one or two things I'd like to discuss with you. Can you spare me some time later in the day?'

'I suppose so, though what you can want with me, I'm not sure. I'll be in the office till one. Come down during the morning if you like.'

'I've got lots to do, so I'll be out in the fields if anyone wants me.'

Jess pulled on wellies and an anorak and left her sister together with the man she had fallen in love with. She gave a slight shudder at this feeling she had so recently discovered. She knew that she really didn't want to go out and leave them together. Everyone always fell for Emily. She was pretty, lively, amusing and although now pregnant, that wouldn't stop her. Jess knew it. No doubt she could even get Drew to fall for her and become the adopted father to her child! There would be nothing she could do to stop it from happening.

When Jess had made a proper assessment of the fire damage, she went back into the house to phone the insurance company. They were somewhat surprised to receive yet another claim from the same person. She could tell that they were about to send some sort of investigator to the farm. Well, so what if they did? The damage had been deliberate, she was certain of it. An investigation was certainly called for.

Emily was out and the car had gone. She must have gone to see Drew, presumably to ask for a job. Jess made some coffee and began to make several lists. She had an urgent need to sort out her finances before she got into any more trouble. She also made a call to the dog breeder.

'Look, I'm really sorry but my sister has come to live with me. She's expecting a baby and there's no way I can manage everything and two pups as well.'

'Don't worry, love,' the breeder replied. 'I've had several new enquiries and there'll be no trouble getting rid of them. I'll even refund your deposit so there's no ill feeling. Maybe you'll have a chance later sometime. I always seem to have some due, what with having three breeding bitches.'

Jess felt relieved, though very disappointed. It was the only sensible thing to do in the circumstances.

Emily arrived back around lunchtime.

'Hi. I've bought us some pasties for lunch. Hope you hadn't prepared anything.'

'Great,' Jess said, surprised at her unexpected thoughtfulness.

'I'm celebrating. Drew's offered me a job, office stuff and so on. Great, isn't it? He's gorgeous, isn't he? And obviously stinking rich. You could do a lot worse, you know.'

'Me? Why should he be interested in me?'

'He is. It shows. And, I think you are also a bit smitten.'

'Don't be silly. I haven't the time for

such things. Much too busy.'

'In that case, you won't mind if I make a move in that direction?'

'Whatever,' Jess managed to mumble.

She felt a jolt in the region of her heart. She really did mind but she didn't have the time to work on any serious relationship. Besides, how could she compete with Em, pregnant or not?

The next couple of weeks were spent in trying to establish some sort of routine for working, keeping house and sorting out the future of the farm. Em disappeared daily to Drew's, most often taking the little car to save the walk down the steep hill. If Jess needed it, she usually drove Emily to work on her way. Though she was making a financial contribution to the house-keeping, Emily did very little to help in the chores. Jess didn't see much of Drew either, until he asked her to have dinner one evening.

'I don't think we have any plans,' she said, assuming Emily was also invited. 'We'd be delighted to accept. Make a change to go out somewhere nice. Did Em suggest any particular day?'

'Er . . . well, I was more thinking of just you and me going out. We haven't seen much of each other lately.'

'But I thought you and Emily . . . well, that you were getting on well. She seems to think so anyhow,' she finished lamely.

'We are, as work colleagues.'

'I see. But you gave her a job, when you didn't really need her so I thought . . . '

'You think too much. Well, are we going to have dinner or not?'

'I don't know how Em will feel about it but provisionally, yes, please. It would be very nice.'

'You're too kind-hearted, Jess. Think of yourself for once. Don't be such a doormat. I never thought of you as giving in to everything your sister wants.'

'I don't. Well, not really. She's in trouble and I try to help as best I can.'

'Not to the extent of giving up your

135

own life, I hope.'

Jess did not reply. She looked thoughtful. Somehow, she always felt the need to try and make up to Em for all sorts of things. Having no parents for a start and lately, for having received the cottage and what little was left of the business.

'Of course not. I haven't been thinking very clearly lately. It's been quite a baptism of fire, you know,' she replied eventually.

'Of course. You've proved yourself but don't let yourself down now.'

'Thanks. OK, name the evening and I'd love to go out with you.'

'Tonight then, and wear something smart. I feel like making it a special occasion.'

He planted an unexpected kiss firmly on her lips and turned to leave.

'I'll pick you up at seven.'

Jess watched him stride up the path and get into his car. She couldn't stop her heart giving a flutter of anticipation. All the same, she knew Emily wasn't going to be very pleased. She'd expect to accompany them and would be most put out that she wasn't included in the invitation.

It was even worse than she'd expected when she broke the news.

'You always get everything, Jess. Everyone likes you because you're just too nice. It isn't fair.'

'I don't want to go there, Em. I'm going out for dinner. Think how many times you've been out without me.'

'That's different. I went out on business quite a lot. You know I had to. It was part of my work.'

'Whatever, but I'm just not prepared to discuss it. I'm going out with Drew. There's plenty of food in the freezer. You can have a quiet night in with the tele and do exactly what you want. Now, I'm going to examine my extensive wardrobe and see what I can find to wear that's decent.'

Emily sat on the sofa and sulked. It really was most unfair. Jess had inherited the entire estate from their grandparents. She had nothing more than a few old bits of jewellery. Jess had the house, and land and any money there was. Whatever she said about there being no money, Emily was sure her sister was exaggerating. Still, she had to admit that she wouldn't want to try and farm this land, even if she had been the inheritor. Jess was foolish even to try. It should have been sold off and split between them. That would have been fair. With a sigh, she picked up the TV guide and began to plan her evening.

Jess came down wearing the only decent dress she had left. It was a midnight blue soft wool with a full skirt. She gave no thought to what was in fashion but she loved the dress.

'You can borrow Gran's sapphire brooch if you like. I know it isn't really sapphire, but it would look good against that colour,' Emily said, having a sudden feeling of guilt about her selfish thoughts.

'Thanks, Em. That's nice of you. I'd

like that. You're certain it isn't real? I thought it was.'

'Doubt it. Take it anyway. It's in the box on my dressing table.'

By seven o'clock, Jess was ready. She realised she only had practical outerwear and lifted down her anorak.

'You can't wear that. Ruins the whole image,' Emily told her.

'Well, I've no choice. I don't have coats for going out.'

'You're hopeless. Hang on. I'll see what I've got. Most of my stuff is still finding its way down here.'

Emily disappeared upstairs and began to rummage through various boxes. She finally reappeared carrying a thick, woollen stole, in varying shades of blues and purples.

'This is the best I can offer but it'll keep you warm in and out of the car.'

'It's gorgeous, thank you. Must have cost you a fortune.'

'Dear Michael gave it to me. I should have thrown the whole lot back at him but one must be practical. Besides, I like it.'

'Oh, Em, you're incorrigible.'

Her sister was a mixture of selfishness and generosity that even Jess found it hard to keep up with.

'You're sometimes such a pain, but I love you dearly.'

The two sisters were hugging each other as Drew knocked at the door. Jess opened it, calling good-night to her sister as she left.

'Was she all right about it?' Drew asked. 'I did feel a bit mean but I can't talk to you with your sister sitting beside us.'

'That sounds ominous,' Jess remarked. 'Anything specific to talk about?'

'We're almost at the restaurant,' he said, avoiding a reply. 'You look nice. I like the brooch. Old, isn't it?'

'It was Gran's. She left it to Em. She kindly loaned it to me for the evening.'

The restaurant was in a small village farther along the coast. It had lots of old beams and a cheery log fire gave a pleasant welcome from the chilly night outside. The whole place had a luxurious air about it. The food smells were delicious but discreet. Leather-bound menus were presented as they sat near the fire sipping cool white wine.

'Wow,' Jess said opening her menu. 'Where does one start on this selection?'

It took a good five minutes merely to read what was on offer.

The dining-room was full but certainly not noisy. Everyone seemed to be concentrating on the excellent food and conversation was minimal. Jess enjoyed the whole occasion and especially the delicious food. Drew had ordered champagne to accompany the succulent fish, caught locally and cooked simply in butter and lemon and flavoured with delicate herbs.

'Why do I deserve champagne?' she asked curiously.

'Because I felt like it. You do like it, don't you?'

'Of course, though I'm not used to drinking it very often.'

'Maybe that could change.'

He looked down for a moment, composing the words in his mind before speaking them.

'Jess, I've grown very fond of you in the last few weeks. I know we haven't actually seen that much of each other but, well, the simple fact is, will you marry me?'

Jess almost choked into the wine glass.

'Marry you? But I hardly know you! We haven't been going out or anything. You don't know me, not the real me.'

'But we like each other. We can have fun. I know it will work. Please, consider it, Jess. Don't just give up on the idea, not without thinking it through.'

'Doesn't love come into the equation?' Jess asked with a touch of sarcasm.

'I'm never entirely sure what love is, but I think I do love you, or I could, given the chance to get to know you better.'

'I think we need to take time before we rush into anything. You know, I can't help thinking that you and Emily would actually be far better suited. There are so many things you have in common.'

'Really? I don't think I care for Emily the way I care for you. Please, think about it, Jess. I'm not such a bad prospect, am I? I'm not that bad looking. I'm not too much older than you are and I'm pretty successful at what I do.'

'There's so much more to marriage than that.'

Her heart was thumping in her chest as she thought of what he was saying to her. She felt certain she loved him but there was no way she was going to enter into any sort of marriage arrangement unless he felt exactly the same way as she did.

'Let's get to know each other better, Drew. I'm very flattered that you asked me but I daren't say yes unless we know each other so well that there are no serious questions or doubts to be answered.'

'Fair enough, I suppose, but if you keep sending me away because you want to be independent, we're never going to get to know each other. You push me away when I try to help and keep refusing any offers I make.'

Somehow, it was difficult to make any polite conversation after that. As they drove home, Drew commented, 'At least you must be giving some consideration to my proposal. You've gone very quiet.'

'I think I may be in shock,' Jess replied with a grin. 'You really are sure you've got the right sister?'

'Quite sure. Please say yes. I shall be waiting for your answer.'

He stopped the car outside Jess's cottage.

'Drew, I like you very much. You know that, but it's too soon.'

'Not for me, Jess. I really do think I love you.'

He leaned over and put his fingers under her chin, lifting her mouth towards his own. Very gently, tenderly and deliberately, he pressed his lips to hers. She felt herself melting towards him. His arms encircled her and he pulled her towards him. Something, maybe her arm, caught the horn and the strident notes sounded out in the clear night air.

'Damn,' she muttered. 'Sorry. Oh, no. I've woken Em.'

The lights went on in the cottage and Em appeared at the window.

'Looks like that's it for now. Do you want to come in for a coffee?'

'I think maybe not. It's quite late and we both have to work tomorrow. I hope you will say yes, however long it takes. Good-night, my dear Jess.'

'Thanks for a lovely evening, and I will think about it, I promise.'

7

Jess was in no mood for talking when she went in. She sent Emily back to bed and quickly went up herself. Sleep was far from her mind as she went over and over Drew's proposal. It seemed out of character for him to be so impulsive, not that it had seemed an impulsive gesture, rather a long, thought about, calculated gesture. Why, she kept asking herself.

Emily was up first the next morning. By the time Jess came down, coffee was already made and bread was ready to pop down in the toaster.

'So, how did it go with the gorgeous Drew?' she demanded. 'My, my, you either drank too much or had to fight him off. You look terrible.'

'I didn't sleep very well, but, yes, it was a nice evening.'

Nice, her thoughts echoed. It was devastating.

'I've been thinking,' Emily began, 'about this farm, Cornwall, the cottage, everything.'

'Oh, yes?'

'What I was thinking was that we could sell up, lock, stock and barrel and put down a deposit on something a bit more central. Maybe not London itself, but somewhere near. It would make sense. You're working yourself into the ground, literally. This place is never going to pay.'

'Haven't you forgotten something? All this talk of we. It is actually mine, though I shall never stop you from living here if you want to, and be realistic, Em. How much do you think we should get for it? It's rundown, not much potential, as you clearly pointed out. We'd be lucky to get a broom cupboard in London with the proceeds. Besides, I don't want to live in London. This is where I want to be. If I can't make the daffodils pay, then I'll try something else. I could grow herbs or specialist vegetables. Forget it, Em. I'm going nowhere. You can please yourself.'

'You're mad, and selfish.'

'And you're a fine one to talk about selfish.'

'I want my share, Jess. You owe it to me.'

'I don't see how I can possibly give you a share, not without selling up and I really don't want to do that. The only way you can have a share is to live here. If it doesn't suit you, then decide where you want to be and go there.'

'What would you say if I told you I might be moving down to the village?'

'I'd be very surprised. Where to exactly?'

'I'm thinking I might move in with Drew. I wondered if that's what he wanted to talk about last night. Sound you out, I mean. You were sort of his friend first, before I came down.'

Jess went red. She felt as if she were choking. Drew had asked her to marry him last night. Now Emily was hinting that there was something between them. She didn't know what to say as Emily continued.

'We've been getting quite close the last week or so. We seem to be on the same wavelength, business-wise at the very least. So you see, you have no real need to stay around here. If you don't want to go to London, find some other little property that would suit you better. Then you can get a job doing something you're good at, instead of turning into some sort of peasant, grubbing a meagre living from a poor bit of land.'

'How dare you, Emily? How dare you try to organise my life? Move out, live with Drew, if he'll have you. Whatever you want you have it, don't you? You've always been spoiled rotten, just because you look pretty and put on your little-girl-lost act. Just get out of my sight.'

The look on her sister's face was almost laughable and if she hadn't felt so wrought, Jess would have laughed out loud.

'OK, I'll go. You don't need the car, do you?' Em said.

'As a matter of fact, I do need my car today. The walk down the hill will do you good. You're pregnant, not an invalid.'

'I take it Drew did speak to you last night and that you didn't like what he had to say.'

Emily swung out of the house before Jess could answer. To calm her anger, she went for a walk round the field. The bulbs were already showing tiny tips of green. She looked at them with pleasure, ignoring the charred mess of the shed and the rusting tractor.

'Oh, Gramps, what should I do? I so wanted to make this work.'

She went back to the cottage and collected her car keys. She drove to Penzance and headed for the library. She wanted to read up some more about growing other crops. Once she had some firm ideas, she could begin to add her sidelines. If she did accept

Drew's marriage proposal, maybe she could still run her project. Granted it may become more of a hobby venture but at least the financial worry would be removed. Maybe she could let the cottage or Emily might choose to live there. She remembered her sister's comments about moving in with Drew. Was that merely her own flight of fancy or was there some truth behind it?

When Emily came back from work, her good humour seemed to have been restored.

'I've got news, sister, dear,' she said brightly.

'Drew's asked you to move in with him?'

Jess forced the words out, though they nearly choked her.

'Well, not exactly, no. I might have solved your problems though. I suggested Drew should buy you out, buy the farm. He could even let you run it as you want to.'

'But why should he do that? It's hardly a good investment.'

'No, but he is considering it. It's the answer, Jess. Your problems would be over. You can pay him rent out of the profits and you'll have oodles of capital left to spend. We might even have ourselves that winter holiday. Invite Drew along, too. What do you think?'

'That you're mad. Selfish as ever but quite mad. What makes you think I'd even consider selling to him? And I don't want to be someone's employee. I think our Mr Rogers can easily decide for himself when and where he invests his money. A failing daffodil farm is not exactly his sort of scene, I think.'

'Well, I've invited him to dinner this evening and he's going to talk about it. You'd better get yourself organised.'

'I assume you are cooking as it's your project. I have things to do.'

Jess flounced off to her room, leaving Emily standing in the kitchen, wondering how to cook anything half decent enough to offer to Drew. There was nothing for it, Emily decided. She would have to cancel. If Jess was persisting on being difficult, there was no point wasting any of their time. She phoned Drew and said Jess wasn't feeling well. He wanted to rush up immediately and send for the doctor but wisely, Emily put him off.

'I'll deal with it. Don't worry. I'm just sorry to have to put you off. Another time perhaps?'

She went up to Jess's room and tapped on the door.

'Can I come in? Jess, please. I've phoned Drew and told him you're not well. He isn't coming.'

'You can come in.'

'I'm sorry, Jess,' Emily said contritely. 'I was only trying to help, really. It seemed like a good idea. Drew was definitely interested. I think he'd do it, for us, if not as a sound investment.'

'It is our home. We were brought up here. Don't you feel anything for it? Gran and Gramps lived here all their married lives. I just can't betray Gramps' trust. He knew how I felt about the place. He knew I'd try and make it live again.'

'I do see, but I hate to see you looking so downtrodden and, well, to put it bluntly, so poor. You deserve better.'

'What exactly is Drew's business?' Jess asked suddenly. 'You work for him. What does his wealth stem from?'

'I gather he was virtually given the hotel by his parents and he'd trained in some financial company. He invested well and reaps the profits.'

'So what do you do there?'

'General secretarial stuff. I manage some of the books for the holiday lets, though that's pretty quiet at this time of year. Still, I'm getting everything sorted and ready for the next season. There are some bookings coming in.'

Jess felt a chill run through her.

'And where exactly are these holiday lets?'

'All over Cornwall. He buys up land apparently and then gets permission to build his chalet places. He seems to have chosen well. Most sites are within spitting distance of the sea. Some are more remote, for the holiday-maker who wants peace and quiet and the rural experience.'

'And that's what is quoted in the brochures?'

'Yes, pretty much.'

'And ailing daffodil farms would make ideal sites, wouldn't they? Especially with access to both the countryside and the sea. Oh, Em, what an idiot I've been.'

'I wouldn't say that.'

'But I see it all now. He wanted to buy the farm and I spoiled all his plans. He'd probably been waiting for Gramps to die so he could put in an offer. He must have organised the unpleasant surprises. I wouldn't even put it past him to have organised the fire, and those two youths he has who help him. He helped me at every turn to avoid my suspicions falling on him. Then when he could see no other way round it, he even tried asking me to marry him. Well, thank heavens, I didn't agree.'

'Drew asked you to marry him? When? Why didn't you tell me?'

'Last night. I told him it was all too soon.'

'And you let me blether on about moving in with him? Oh, Jess, you must think I'm an absolute idiot.'

'You are, Emily, but I love you all the same. You're always too wrapped up in your own agenda to think of anyone else.'

'Now I sound horrible as well. How do you put up with me? So what do we do now? Go and face him?'

'No. You continue working for him for the time being and see exactly what you can find out. Go through the files and anything else you have access to. I have to know the truth.'

They spent the evening planning and scheming and actually began to enjoy themselves. They even managed to laugh at several pieces of their own misunderstandings. During the night, the weather broke and their sleep was interrupted by the crashing of thunder and torrential rain.

Poor daffodils, Jess thought. But they must have survived worse than this in the past, she tried to comfort herself.

The next morning was still wet, though not quite so much rain as the previous night. Emily went off to work in the car and Jess pulled on wellies and a long, waterproof coat. She had to see the damage that must have been caused by the torrential rain in the night. She plodded out through the water-soaked garden and into the field. She didn't need to go very far before she could see the standing water that covered the entire field.

She felt tears running down her cheeks. The entire crop of bulbs was under water. They could never survive this drenching, she thought. Those tender green shoots she had noticed earlier were totally submerged. But maybe, if the rain stopped and one of the drying winds began, they might just pull round.

'Oh, Gramps,' she whispered aloud,

'what should I do now?'

Maybe there was something wrong with the drainage. Perhaps there was something Gramps did to prevent such flooding. There was nothing she could do about it at this time. It was a case of wait and see, something she'd never been good at doing.

She spent a desultory day, vaguely trying to plan her next move. All thoughts of marrying Drew had to be forgotten. She didn't know just how much Emily's flights of fancy were in her imagination or based on reality.

If Drew was willing to offer to marry Jess to get his hands on the farm, he could easily have been working on her sister, too. Jess thought about the man. He was kind. He had a good sense of humour. He seemed to show real caring and when he had kissed her, it was tenderness itself. How could she even think that he could be so underhand? Surely, she wasn't such a rotten judge of character. She felt her eyes pricking with tears.

'Oh, Drew,' she moaned out loud. 'Can I have been so wrong?'

She didn't want to believe he had ulterior motives, but dare she take the risk?

'There's planning applications in for several sites in the area but as far as I can see, nothing for this particular bit of land,' Emily announced when she came home that evening. 'And Drew was quite sympathetic when I told him about your reaction. Said he wasn't surprised. So, the deal to buy the farm is off.'

'How can you be so casual about it all?' Jess demanded.

'No point worrying about something that isn't going to happen. So, what next?'

'Tell me honestly, Em, has Drew made any advances towards you?'

'Not as such, but he wouldn't, would he? Not if he likes you.'

'So what made you think of moving in with him?'

'Dunno really. Just speculating.

What's for supper?'

And that was it, as far as Emily was concerned. Jess half wished she could be more like her sister. She always seemed to manage to push things to one side and get on with the next task.

'I begin to think the only way out the mess is to leave you here and let you make what you can of life, maybe with Drew,' Emily said. 'I'll simply make another fresh start, somewhere else. Maybe go abroad for a while.'

Jess felt quite depressed at the turn her plans had taken. If there really was no way she could make her living with daffodils, what with the weather and the world conspiring against her, she might as well give up now, before things got any worse. If someone did develop the land, it would mean a substantial amount of money which she could share with Emily. After all, she was going to need sufficient money to bring up a baby single-handed.

'Jess, you can't,' Emily burst out when Jess revealed her thoughts. 'What about your dreams, your plans? What would Gramps have thought? He was relying on you.'

'You've changed your tune. I thought it was what you wanted.'

'Not any more, not now I've seen you here and how hard you work. Give it time, please, Jess. I do believe that Drew loves you, too. He's been very hard-going today.'

'I'm not so sure about that. OK, I'll try to keep things going for this season. We won't make much money out of the crop, if any at all, but we'll give it a go. We'll find a way of making enough to live on somehow.'

The two girls hugged each other, both intent on the new plan.

8

Jess worked hard over the coming months. As Emily's pregnancy advanced, she gave up working for Drew but she did contribute financially to the household expenses. She felt tired much of the time and relied on Jess more and more as the months went by.

Christmas came and went. Drew invited them both for the day and Mrs Jamieson provided a splendid spread, no expense spared. He was the perfect host and gave them both generous gifts of expensive sweaters, scarves and warm hats. They felt slightly embarrassed by the lavishness when all they had brought was wine and chocolates.

Apart from that, Jess avoided seeing Drew as much as possible. He had given up asking her for a decision and seemed to have accepted the situation.

There was a cold snap in late

January, setting back the picking season by a few weeks. The urgency of getting flowers out at the earliest possible moment to get the best prices was lost, but as the same thing had happened to all the growers in the area, it might not prove too great a disaster. Jess spent the days watching anxiously for the first flowers. The new shed had been installed, thanks to Drew's contacts, and the prompt payment from the insurance company. All she needed now was for some decent weather and she could begin the next stage of the work.

She went back into the kitchen and found the dishes from breakfast still on the table.

'Oh, Em, you could at least have done the washing up,' she complained. 'I know you're tired but surely you could have managed that.'

'Sorry, Jess. I don't feel so good.'

'What's wrong?'

'I don't know. I feel slightly strange.'

'Is it the baby, do you think?'

'I'm not sure.'

'I'd better get the doctor.'

'I'll be OK. It's another six weeks before it's due. I'll just rest for a while and I'm sure I'll be fine.'

'If you're sure. I'll get some lunch and maybe you should go to bed. We'll see how you are a bit later.'

Jess heated a can of soup and made some toast and took them up the narrow stairs to Emily's room. She looked pale and very tired. She made an attempt to eat her soup but obviously was struggling with it. Jess frowned, wondering what she should do but Em was adamant that she did not need medical attention.

'I'd just like to sleep if it's OK with you. I shall be better after a decent rest. I was awake a lot last night. Couldn't get comfortable.'

'If you're sure. I'll leave your mobile phone by the bed and you must call me if you need me. I'll probably stay around the house anyhow, but just in case, I'll have mine in my pocket.'

Em nodded her agreement and Jess left her to rest.

By evening, Emily was feeling better. She came down, proclaiming that the sleep had done her the world of good.

'We really ought to get things in for the baby,' Jess said after supper. 'You never know if it might come early. We'd be high and dry. Let's go into town tomorrow and get the basics.'

'It almost seems like tempting fate,' Em replied, 'but you're probably right. You usually are.'

But plans changed dramatically during the night. Jess awoke to hear Emily yelling and rushed through to her room.

'The baby, Jess. I think it's coming.'

She lay back against the pillow, white with pain and beaded with perspiration.

'I woke suddenly and well, ouch . . . '

She panted again, obviously in the throes of a contraction.

'Hang on in there. I'll call the doctor, midwife, everyone.'

She rushed to the phone but there

was no sound. The line was down! She cursed and grabbed her mobile and punched in the number.

'I'm afraid the doctor's out on an emergency. I'll try to get hold of him but I can't promise how long he'll be,' the answering service said.

Jess called the midwife. She, too, was out and the next on the list was even farther away. She called for an ambulance and cursed she hadn't done that first. In desperation, she called Drew's number. Sleepily, he answered.

'Drew, please can you come! Emily's in labour and I can't get help. If you can come, at least you can do the boiling water bit and keep trying the phone. Must dash.'

She'd heard Emily groaning again and unlocked the front door, before rushing back up the stairs.

'I want to go to the loo,' Emily moaned, 'but I can't get out of bed.'

Jess remembered there were various things left over from when Gran was nursed and she hunted in the back of a cupboard to find them. There were a number of useful things like rubber sheets and a bedpan. She grabbed everything and added towels and spare sheets to the pile. She desperately tried to remember everything they had read together about labour and birth, wishing they'd read it again more recently. If only the ambulance would come, but the narrow lanes were probably blocked with a recent snowfall and it would take ages to get through. From the look of her sister, it wouldn't be in time.

The room felt chilly, so Jess found a heater and put it on full before she lifted the covers off Em's bed. Calmly, she took control, praying as she did so that everything would be all right. When Drew arrived, he came straight into the room, no thoughts for modesty or anything else.

'How is she?' he asked.

'OK, but it's nearly coming, I'm sure.'

'OK, let's get to work.'

To both girls' amazement, he seemed

to know exactly what to do and before long, a tiny baby girl was lying in Jess's arms, wrapped in a towel. Em suddenly fainted and lay motionless for several minutes.

'Oh, what's wrong? Emily,' Jess called, 'Emily. Come back to us.'

She carefully laid the baby down in a nest made between two pillows and bent over her sister anxiously. She put a flannel on her face and tried to bring her back to consciousness. At last her eyes fluttered and opened.

'Thank goodness,' Jess gasped. 'Are you all right?'

'My baby,' Em mumbled. 'I thought I heard it cry but it didn't, did it? Oh, and I wanted it so much.'

'Of course nothing's wrong. It's a little girl. She's lovely, and fine.'

She handed the precious bundle to her sister and felt tears rushing down her cheeks.

'Don't worry, Em. We'll both give her the best possible start. I'll help you with her.'

Mother and child lay together quietly. Em examined every tiny finger, marvelling at the tiny ears and the bunched-up, little face.

'How on earth did you know what to do, Drew?' Jess gasped when the panic was over.

'I helped my grandfather on his farm. I reckoned the process was similar enough for sheep and humans.'

'I'm glad I know that,' Emily murmured.

They heard sounds from downstairs and Jess ran down to see who it was. Two ambulance men were coming into the cottage carrying medical bags and a folding chair.

'She's got a girl. She's very tiny, though. Six weeks early, we reckoned.'

Jess was babbling on without thinking properly.

'Will you take her to hospital?'

'We certainly will. My, you live in a lonely spot. Took us ages to find it, and the road's blocked for the last bit. Couldn't get the ambulance through.

We had to walk quite a long way.'

They went upstairs to see the patient and were most complimentary about the way everything had been dealt with.

'Just as well,' one of them said as he finished examining mother and child. 'If you'd waited for us, I doubt either of them would be in such good shape.'

'Do I have to go to hospital?' Emily asked.

'We must get the baby checked properly and a feeding routine established. She's very tiny. Have you got clothes for her?'

'We were going tomorrow,' Jess told them feebly.

'Well, Dad luckily knew what to do,' he said cheerfully, mistaking Drew for the father. 'Congratulations, sir.'

'But . . . ' Emily protested.

'Do you want to come in with them? I think you'd best drive separately. Follow us through the lanes and then you'll be able to get back again, unless Auntie wants to drive your car.'

The confusion was just too much to

try to explain so they let it go.

'You go with Em, Drew, and I'll follow with some things she'll need. It's too late to think of sleep now. It's the next day already and I do have some shopping to do,' Jess said quickly.

The next few days passed in a whirl of activity, with visits to the hospital, preparing for the baby's return home and trying to keep a check on the business. Jess felt exhausted even before they'd really had any responsibility for the baby. Emily was kept in hospital for a longer than the normal time, as the child wasn't yet feeding properly.

'I'm just useless,' she said on several occasions. 'I was never built for motherhood.'

'I promised you, I'll do my best to help with her,' Jess kept repeating. 'Between us, we'll be fine.'

As the weeks passed, the baby thrived and the two sisters found a routine that seemed to work. The flower-picking season had begun and Jess was out at all hours, organising the small team of local housewives who had come to pick every year. The bank balance grew satisfactorily but she would certainly need to diversify if the whole thing was to survive long-term.

Drew was a frequent visitor to the cottage and seemed to enjoy his time spent with the tiny baby, now growing well. Emily had decided to call her Andrea, in his honour. She even suggested he might like to be a godparent, along with Jess. He was delighted and immediately began planning ways to help in the future.

'Whoa, there,' Jess told him. 'No way will she be going to some expensive boarding school, as you suggest. This child will always know the love of a good home.'

'Oh, I do agree,' he said with a grin. 'Besides, I'm not sure if I can do without seeing her for a whole term at a time.'

Jess thought about his words later. He seemed very fond of both Emily and the baby and she felt a little left out. It was a good job she had never taken his marriage proposal seriously. It would have been a disaster. It could even be that he and Em would get married in time and she would have the cottage and business all to herself again.

She wasn't entirely sure she could cope with that. She still felt very deeply for this man but knew she'd lost her chance of happiness with him. What a mixture of emotions teemed through her mind. Did she care enough about her sister to give away her own chances of happiness with Drew?

As things moved along into some sort of routine, Emily went back to work for Drew two mornings a week while Jess looked after her tiny niece. She adored the baby and looked forward to the times she spent alone with her.

A large envelope arrived one morning when she was on baby-minding duties. She ripped it open and read the contents with growing disbelief. A speculative builder wanted to buy the farm and land for development for new homes, especially affordable starter homes for local people. The figure offered made her senses reel. She considered the implications and realised that it would be the answer to everything, once she could square her conscience with her grandfather's memory.

There should be enough money to buy a decent house, big enough for the three of them and leave something over to live on for a while at least. It was very tempting. She looked at the name of the company but it was no-one she had heard of. The address was a head office address in London. Obviously, it was a cover for someone local. She didn't need too long to guess who that someone was.

As soon as Emily returned, she would go into town and look them up in the company directory. She would also go to the planning office and see if she could find out anything there. She could try pumping Em but felt that she might do better having the facts before her officially. She carefully folded the letter and draft agreement forms and packed them away in her handbag. She planned to say nothing to her sister until she had more facts.

Emily was curious about her sister's sudden need to go to town but said nothing.

'Will you be away long, Jess?' she asked.

'Dunno. Be back for supper anyhow. Depends how it goes. See you.'

'But lunch, what about lunch?' she called after the retreating figure. 'Now, Andrea, are you going to tell me what all that was about?' she said, lifting her little girl out of the carrycot. 'What's come over Auntie Jess?'

She went for a rummage round the filing cabinet later, but could find nothing significant.

Jess's trip was not much help. The company seemed to be genuine and there was nothing given to indicate any involvement with one Andrew Rogers. The planning office was unhelpful. She requested an interview but was told the appropriate officer was out for the day. She asked if it was possible to obtain any form of planning consent on land not owned by an applicant. It appeared possible, but not without the owner's consent.

Perhaps Gramps had been thinking along those lines before he died. She asked how difficult it would be to get consent for developing land overlooking the sea. She was told that in general it was rarely granted due to conservation rules but in the case of special housing, low-cost starter homes, in a quiet area, there would definitely be a possibility.

'And of course,' the planning officer continued, 'there are the grants available to keep the costs low. There's always a shortage of homes for local people. People from up-country like to buy up anything going for holiday homes. Then prices escalate and we're back to square one.'

'Thanks very much. You've been a

great help,' Jess said as she left.

It now seemed clear. The speculator had obviously been along this route. If he was willing to spend the money, maybe she should contemplate such a scheme herself. It was certainly worth considering.

As Jess drove home, she remembered the man she had seen looking over and measuring the field, soon after her arrival. He was someone Drew knew so she veered off and stopped outside Drew's house. He seemed delighted to see her and took her into the lounge. Mrs Jamieson appeared with tea, as if my magic.

'This is an unexpected pleasure,' Drew told her. 'I'd almost come to think you've been avoiding me.'

'Busy, that's all. Look, I wanted to ask your help, your advice. I've had an offer for the land and the cottage.'

She watched his face carefully but there was nothing to indicate he knew anything about the deal.

'But I thought you'd never sell.'

'It's a very generous offer. I wondered if that guy who was here one day, ages ago, if he might have anything to do with it.'

Drew looked blank.

'Green car, came to see you.'

'Oh, Wayne Drury. You remember him. He went to the village school. Several years older than us. He runs the estate agencies around the place.'

'Good heavens! Yes, I do remember him. I thought he looked familiar when I saw him but I'd never have guessed.'

'He's rather a dodgy character. Always doing shady deals if the reports are true. My two lads work for him at times.'

'Do they now. Helping me that day would have been a good chance to spy out the land. So what was he doing with you?'

'Came to ask me to be a part of some deal, but naturally, I said no. I couldn't afford to be associated with anyone like him. I sent him packing, but he could be involved in something.'

'So he could have been responsible for the break-ins? And maybe the fire?'

'Wouldn't put it past him. He wouldn't do it himself but he'd certainly be capable of finding someone local to organise it all. The two lads for instance?'

'Wow. I'd almost begun to think I'd imagined it was directly targeted at me. I even wondered if you were involved, Drew.'

'Jess, how could you? I'd never do anything to hurt you. I love you, Jess. I've really missed seeing you these last few months. You had become very important to me.'

'I'm sorry. It was just that you were always around when things went wrong, and then when Emily arrived, you seemed to like her. Everyone seems to fall for Emily and I'm just the one in the background who doesn't get noticed.'

'Oh, my darling girl. I've been trying so hard to keep my distance. I thought you didn't love me and, well, I didn't want to make any more of a fool of myself.'

'But you seemed so in charge when Andrea was born. You even looked pleased when the ambulance people called you the dad.'

'It was all a bit emotional that night. No, Jess, it's you I love and always have. Do you have any feelings for me? Is there a chance for me?'

'Oh, Drew, of course there is. I didn't dare to believe that you could truly love me. That proposal you made, months ago, you didn't seem as if you knew then.'

'I didn't know how to say it, and yes, on reflection, you were right to want to wait. I didn't know my own mind really. Let's start again, shall we? Let's really get to know each other.'

'Yes, please,' Jess whispered as he took her in his arms and kissed her as tenderly as she remembered from the first time he kissed her.

A cough from the doorway interrupted.

'Excuse me. I'm sorry to interrupt. I came to see if you'd finished with the tea things. Will you be dining at home this evening, sir, or will you be having a guest?' Mrs Jamieson enquired.

She definitely had a twinkle in her eye, Jess realised.

'I think we'll probably be going out thanks. We may be celebrating.'

'That's very gratifying, sir, ma'am.'

When the housekeeper had left the room, Jess giggled.

'She's a little bit Dickens, isn't she? Sir, ma'am, honestly.'

'She's been used to working here all her life. When it was a hotel she had a staff to manage. Old habits die hard. Now, where shall we go to eat?'

'Em's expecting me. I rushed out with scarcely a word at lunchtime.'

'How about I get a takeaway and we'll share it together over some wine?'

'Better go and warn Em first. She might just have spent hours cooking up something. She'd never forgive us if we took food in that was better.'

'You are joking, aren't you? I didn't think Emily could cook. She's brilliant in the office but cooking is definitely not her strength.'

They didn't need to worry. Em was still in the process of wondering which pack of ready meals she would take out of the freezer and was delighted at the prospect of being spared the need to cook anything at all. When Drew left to collect the food, she looked quizzically at her sister.

'So, what's been going on, Jess? You look like the cat that got the cream. Why so mysterious all of a sudden?'

'I had an offer for the land and cottage and needed to check out who was behind it. I called on Drew on the way back and he offered to take me out but I thought it might be nicer to have a night at home, all together.'

'Doesn't explain that glint in your eye. There's something more, isn't there?'

'Not really, and before you ask, no,

I'm not going to sell Gramps' daffodil farm.'

When Drew returned, he was carrying the hot food and a bottle of champagne as well as wine.

'Thought we'd have a little celebration,' he said popping the cork.

'Am I particularly stupid or something? What exactly are we celebrating?' Emily asked.

'To Andrea,' Jess said raising a glass.

They all drank to the baby.

'And to what else?' Emily demanded again. 'Come on, guys, what's going on?'

'To life and the future,' Drew toasted.

'I give up. To life and the future, whatever it may bring. You know, I never thought I'd say it, but motherhood is having a profound effect on me. I actually feel contented with life for once. I've probably got less around me in material things but it's people who count.'

Emily looked happy and Jess hugged her.

'It's good to see you looking settled. Have you told Michael by the way? He should know he's got a daughter.'

'No, I haven't told him and don't intend doing so. No point. Andrea is our little baby, yours and mine and Drew's, if he wants to be associated with her. He did act as midwife after all.'

When the meal was over, Drew asked Jess to accompany him out to the daffodil field.

'They're mostly dying off now. There isn't much to see. I've started lifting some of the bulbs to dry,' Jess explained.

'I'd still like to see the field,' he told her.

They walked out into the darkness, lit by a sliver of moon. Stars were shining overhead in great profusion.

'I'd hate to live in a city again. You can't see this spectacle where street lights are too bright.'

Drew pulled her towards him.

'Will you marry me, Jess? I love you so much.'

'I will, but not until the field is full of daffodils again.'

'But that's months away.'

'Yes, but I want my own daffodils in my bouquet. Sentimental old fool, I know, but somehow, I know it's what Gran and Gramps would have wanted.'

'Funny girl. It also gives us time to plan things. We have to make sure we know who was really responsible for the damage and thefts from your cottage, and we'll see about this company who wants your land. I'm sure Wayne Drury is involved in it and the two lads. Nobody is going to do anything that could jeopardise your crop for the next season. We need every single daffodil we can get, to cover the church, the reception, the coach, the bridesmaids and you, of course. I'm making certain I don't lose you a second time.'

'Now who's the romantic one?' Jess asked happily.

'And you will move down to live in the big house, won't you, when we're married? I don't think I could cope in the small space of your place. But then, Emily can live in the cottage and you'll see her every day when you go to tend your precious daffodils.'

'Exactly how long have you been planning all this? It sounds as if you've got everything worked out.'

'Dreaming about it for ages. I just needed to finalise the details.'

'What, like me agreeing to it all?'

He nodded.

'And can I have two Jack Russell pups, like I'd planned?'

'Do you know something, Jessica Farley? You talk too much. Now, where were we?'

He kissed her once more and held her close.

'I can think of nothing nicer than daffodils for a bride.'